The Only Cellar

The Only Cellar

Paul Larralde

To order additional copies of this book, contact:
Xlibris LLC
1-888-795-4274
www.Xlibris.com
Orders@Xlibris.com
622857

Dedication

This work is dedicated to my wife and family,
they were subjected to many
weird ideas and opinions.
Also to my sister Grace for her help and editing.

country (the provinces of Biscay and Guipuscoa) into which, since the arrival of the auxiliaries, they had never penetrated; the result was, as in the former experiments they had made, that they were obliged to retreat back to Vittoria. So that now they are reduced to the necessity of going this circuitous route, unless they make a more successful effort to open the road, which I have very strong reasons to disbelieve. Meanwhile, day by day, the infantry of Don Carlos augments, in more rapid proportion than the forces of the enemy melt away, and the state of the case may be summed up in these few words. The force of Don Carlos is too great in Biscay, Navarre, and Guipuscoa, for all the Queen's troops, including the auxiliaries, and all that Mendizabal will ever get together of his levée en masse, to dislodge him. If it is attempted, they will meet with nothing but defeat and destruction.

The army of Don Carlos, on the other hand, from want of cavalry, will never (if the Queen's continue in its present state) be able to cross the Ebro and advance along the plains of Castille, without incurring the same penalty. Furthermore, Don Carlos cannot raise sufficient cavalry in those provinces. The country produces none, and the expense and difficulty of getting more than enough to supply accidental deficiencies from France is too great. The advance on Madrid will, therefore, probably be made from the eastern provinces of Catalonia and Valencia; the former of which is in the same state as the Basque provinces were a year ago; the latter as in the commencement of the war; and here any number of cavalry may be raised. The insurgents, whose organisation is proceeding slowly, and can only be accelerated by the arrival of repeated divisions from the camp of Don Carlos, are, however, too strong to give the Queen's government any chance of checking them, by any force which it has now in, or which it can send to, those provinces, without abandoning, or so much weakening its defence of Castille, that it would leave the shorter road open to him, by which he might proceed at once to the capital. Thus, slowly, events must work their way, and the Queen has no remedy

Chapter One

Spring was trying to come early to the foothills and plains of Eastern Colorado. Today, however, the warmth was being bounced all over the place by a forty- to fifty-mile-per-hour wind.

I was headed home from my job early. Due to economic times, the company I worked for did not want to pay any overtime. To get the coverage of help they wanted, each hourly employee had to take time off during the week when it was their Saturday to work a half day.

I worked as a farm equipment mechanic, and spring was always slow. Once in a while, getting a little time off and being able to do some business that couldn't be handled on the weekends was even better.

On my way home, I saw five head of deer huddled in a pasture between two houses. *I bet they are as sick of this wind as I am.* They did not seem too concerned with the traffic or the horses that were in the pasture next to them.

Arriving at home, I was greeted by our two dogs. These animals stay in the house while my wife and I are at work. The house has air-conditioning in the summer and heat in the winter. Sometimes I think there is something wrong with this picture; their living conditions are a lot better than my working conditions. They are great pets, and I probably wouldn't have it any other way.

I checked the answering machine as I entered the kitchen, and there was one call. Whoever had called had not left a message. *Probably wants to sell me something I don't need or want.*

I just turned away from the phone when it rang. The ring startled me a little, but I quickly recovered. From the double ring on the phone, I knew this call was a long-distance call, and it was probably my son in Denver. I answered after the second ring and was greeted by a pleasant female voice. She said her name quickly and then told me she worked for a law office. She rattled the name very fast.

I am sure she says the name of the firm a hundred times a day. She asked if I would hold for a call from Leslie Flemmings, quickly thanked me, and put me on hold.

Telemarketers, I thought to myself and was ready to hang up when another female voice came on the line. She introduced herself as Leslie Flemmings, and she was a senior partner in the law firm of mumbo jumbo mumbo jumbo. She also was used to saying the firm's name very fast, and the only name that made sense to me was Flemmings. She continued on to explain she needed to meet with me as soon as possible and wanted to know if tonight would be open. She reiterated that a prompt meeting was needed. She explained the meeting was in reference to a case she was working on and was sure I hadn't heard anything about the situation. She further explained the action had something to do with me, but she was unable to explain further over the phone.

I agreed to meet with her that evening at the Hilton on the south end of town at 7:00 p.m. She said she would meet me in the lobby, to check at the front desk in case her plane was late. She thanked me and hung up.

She left me feeling as if I had been hit by a tornado. This feeling would happen many more times before all of this "case" was settled.

I spent the rest of the day doing some odd jobs around the house and wondering just what I had agreed to. I still had the feeling the deal was some type of sales pitch and before the meeting was over, she would be asking for money. I hadn't gotten her phone number, so I couldn't call back and tell her to cancel the meeting, but I felt very uneasy about the whole thing.

At five o'clock, my wife arrived from work, and we discussed her day. I told her the story of the phone call and the meeting that had been arranged for this evening. She seemed interested but was also skeptical about the purpose of the appointment and its urgency. She told me to leave the checkbook at home, as well as my credit cards.

I cleaned up and had supper before heading to the Hilton. If the traffic was decent, it would still take me twenty minutes to get there. Rush hour could extend past seven o'clock pretty easily, and I didn't want to be too late for this "urgent meeting."

Chapter Two

I arrived about ten minutes early at the parking lot of the Hilton. Traffic had been crazy, but I still made good time.

I decided to go inside and see if Leslie was around. The sooner I got this over, the better. I approached the front desk and inquired about the lawyer. The clerk replied she was seated in the corner table and was waiting for me. My walking across the lobby area must have gotten her attention because as I approached, she stood up and gave me a friendly smile.

She introduced herself but acted as if she was real sure who I was. She appeared to be in her forties and was definitely stocky built. Her short stature of about five foot two was accented by the spare forty to sixty pounds she was carrying. She had a pleasant face and wore very stylish glasses. Her face showed gentleness but also looked as if she could be very stern.

A fairly quick exchange of formalities, and she was ready to get down to business. She told me a little about herself and how long she had been with the law firm. At this point, she began the tale of a lifetime.

She explained that her firm represented a man who had passed away and had left his entire estate to me.

With this information, I was already thinking the next thing this woman was going to say was something to the effect of "If you will give us a cashier check for a few thousand dollars, he could finish the case, and I would get my money."

This was not the case, however, or at least not yet. She continued on with the information, but I still was very skeptical.

Leslie explained her client was a young man in the early seventies. He was traveling through Colorado on his way to Nevada to interview for a job.

Outside of Glenwood Springs, he had some car trouble. It took all the money he had to have his car towed and repaired. He was headed out of town, and the car ran out of gas, so he decided to walk back to town to try and find some help. A young man in a Dodge Ramcharger stopped and picked him up. He listened to the traveler's story and told him he would take him to the nearest gas station. When they arrived at the station, the traveler asked the driver if he had a ten he could spare. All the driver had was a twenty, and he gave it to the traveler.

The traveler borrowed a gas can from the gas station, and the man in the Ramcharger returned him to his car. During the trip back, the traveler told the driver his story about trying to get to Nevada for a job interview. When they arrived at the stalled car, the driver gave him another twenty and said he would need it to get to Nevada. The traveler said he would pay it back and got out of the truck. The driver yelled "good luck" and drove off.

Her client got to Nevada on the forty dollars and got the job with a firm that specialized in government building projects.

I just sat there, amazed at how accurate this account of that day was. When I had picked up the hitchhiker and he told me his story, I knew I was out twenty bucks. Why I gave him the additional twenty dollars that day was beyond me, but I did it anyway. When I let him off at his car, I knew I would never see him or my money again. At the time, I was sure he would never pay it back. He didn't get my name or address before I left.

Leslie interrupted my thoughts as she progressed on with her story. The traveler got the job and worked for this company for fifteen years before he bought the company from the owner who was retiring. He continued to do government construction, most being of the top-secret high-paying type and accumulated enough money to purchase a place in Western Colorado. This place was also owned by the man who owned the company.

After a few more years, he sold his construction business and settled on this property. Since he had no family and all of his friends had more money than they could spend, he decided to return a kindness done to him and kept his word that he would pay it back.

"This is the reason for this meeting," Leslie said. "My boss and associate, Christopher, passed away two years ago from cancer. His wish was that before his will was settled, any and all objections or arguments would be settled. Also, all taxes and expenditures would be handled. When this inheritance was handed over, it would be as free and clear as the forty dollars was in 1976."

As Leslie paused, my mind raced on with all the skeptic thoughts I could come up with. The story was accurate and true. Only one other person besides me was involved. The inheritance really sounded too good to be true, and I still kept expecting someone to ask me for money so this transaction would be complete. That time, however, would never come.

A couple of things made all of this so real. First, I have only picked up a couple of hitchhikers in my whole life. Second, I very seldom carry cash and really rarely have money on my person. Maybe generosity to an unknown hitchhiker was destiny, but someone would have to prove the concept to me.

My first question to her was "How did he find me and my name and address?"

"Christopher used his many contacts from doing government contracting to track you down a long time ago and to keep track of you. He was able to get any information he wanted like your social security number and credit history with his contacts in the government."

She didn't say more other than it has happened for years and if a person is not trying to hide, they can be found quite easily and quickly. The first clue, however, was he got my license plate number before I left him at his car alone. His intent was to return the money as soon as possible but never got around to doing it.

I sat back in my chair and tried to absorb all of this and what it meant. My thoughts were bouncing here and there. Some good, some extravagant, and of course, my skeptic, cautious side, was rearing its head.

Leslie continued to talk and release information about Christopher and his abilities to keep up with me. My mind seemed to be saturated with all these thoughts like *Is this legitimate? How many other people have this information? How will this change my life? How much is the estate?* These thoughts bounced around like a giant beach ball.

What she was saying sounded like a big BS story, yet she had information that no other person would know. If I had been asked to describe the occasion, I would not have given such an accurate account of this chance meeting in 1976. I do remember telling my wife about the incident when I got home that night. She asked me why I had given him so much money, and I didn't have a good reason.

Finally, my mind was satisfied, and I came back to reality. Leslie was going over a typed piece of paper and not really noticing whether I was paying attention or not.

The paper was a receipt for a small package she had set out in front of her. I looked at the receipt and noticed all the names of the law firm printed on the letterhead. The receipt did not say what was in the package. All I needed to do was sign and I could find out.

I signed the paper, and as per her recommendation, I didn't open the package. Leslie did state she was not sure what was in the package. There was a short pause in the output of information from her, but the lull did not last long.

Leslie continued with the business at hand. She told me I needed to go to the courthouse for the final reading and dispersal of the will. The courthouse she referred to was across the state.

I figured about an eight-hour drive from here, but she told me that it was an-hour-and-a-half plane ride. She wanted to know if I could meet her at the local airport in the morning about seven o'clock. Then, as if she had a brainstorm, she said she would come and pick me up at my home at seven o'clock. My first thought was *This lady is nuts*, but decided I better take the time now to get this inheritance straightened out. I told her I would be ready at seven o'clock. She told me I would need a couple of days for this initial meeting, so I should bring a night bag.

"My boss will be real happy to hear that," I stated. "A very quiet time of the year and will save him payroll."

Today was Wednesday, so if I were gone for two days, I would be back for my turn to work on Saturday morning. There was a remote chance this inheritance would be big enough that we may be able to retire. *Now that would be a great thought.* I told her the morning would be fine, and I would give her directions to my house.

She said, "That won't be necessary, I know where you live." With that statement, she closed her briefcase, shook my hand, and headed out the door.

I just sat there for a few minutes before rising and heading to my pickup. I almost forgot the package, but remembered it just at the last minute.

I took the fastest way home and couldn't wait to drop this bomb on my wife and see her reaction. I glanced at the package and wondered what type of "treasure" it contained. The bundle lay in the seat next to me, quite harmless looking. The closer to home I got, the more the thought bothered me that I hadn't opened it. Maybe a Pandora"s Box. By the time I got home, the bundle really had almost all of my attention and was almost like I had to open the bundle right now. I felt like a small child waiting to open his only Christmas present.

Chapter Three

I got out of my pickup and picked up the package. In this day and age, the package may be a bomb. I carried the package as if it may very well be a bomb.

I walked into the house and set the bundle on the kitchen table. After sharing a little conversation with my wife, I had to open the package. If it was a Pandora's Box, I wanted to know tonight, not tomorrow on the plane ride to an undisclosed destination across the state.

I cut the tape seal and carefully opened the package. Inside, there was a sealed brown envelope, the type that is about eight-by-twelve inches with a metal tab on the back. I slowly opened the metal tabs and found that the inside was full of money. Bills were packed so tight, I don't think you could get another one in there. Also, there was a note from Christopher.

The note was short and to the point. It stated the enclosed envelope contained the forty dollars I had loaned him some thirty odd years ago, plus a little extra to cover the interest for the years since the loan.

I started to count the bills and quickly found they were one-hundred-dollar bills. All of them were one-hundred-dollar bills!

My wife and I started to stack them in piles of ten. Soon, stacks covered the kitchen table. When our task was complete, there were forty piles. We just sat there for a few minutes and recounted. There were two twenty-dollar bills by themselves. Christopher had definitely paid back his debt.

Taking a little time to collect our senses, I began to tell my wife about the meeting and how I would be taking a plane ride across the state in the morning to go to a courthouse somewhere to hear "the rest of the story." I had a feeling I knew where we would end up, but I wasn't sure. I told her all the information Leslie had given me. The trip tomorrow was to get all the paperwork finished. I was not sure what else was included in the estate, if anything, but my signature and presence were required. She agreed now was the time to "get this over with."

We again looked through the money to make sure we hadn't counted wrong. Forty thousand dollars in cash is quite a sight to see sitting on your kitchen table. The stacks were more than I make working my tail off for the whole year. We put the money back in the envelope and put it in the desk drawer. I reread the note a couple of times and finally put it in the drawer.

We talked about the estate probably being a "money pit" and the forty thousand would go fast. Slowly, doubt started to creep in and wonderment followed. We would both have to get two jobs to pay back taxes, inheritance tax, and lawyer fees. The forty thousand was a step in the right direction, hopefully enough to cover most of the expenses.

I called the owner of the place where I work and left him a message that I needed a couple of days off. Since business was slow, a couple of days should not leave them too much in a bind. I told him I would call tomorrow and let him know more.

After a couple of hours trying to get to sleep, we finally dozed off, and neither of us slept very well. I found myself awake a couple of times in the night. Finally, we were greeted by the dogs and got up about our normal time.

Leslie arrived on time, and I introduced her to my wife. They exchanged formalities, and the dogs just about mauled her to get her attention for some pets and pats. She freely gave them both most of the attention they requested and then stated we should head to the airport, and I would be returning here in a couple of days. She quickly inserted the company plane was waiting.

With a quick goodbye to my wife, we loaded into the car and were off to the airport. As we arrived, Leslie took the car past some hangars and slightly onto the tarmac. There sat a King Air, red and white in color. The twin-engine turboprop appeared to have been "spit shined" as we were coming to get on the plane. It was a beautiful sight to see such a pretty plane.

The door was open, and two men in casual dress were standing near the plane. Leslie informed me that these men were the pilots. We walked up to the first man, and she introduced him as Mr. Andrew Robbes, the pilot. The copilot was Mr. John Flemmings, her husband.

We all boarded, and I was informed the flight would take about an hour and a half. I asked where we were going, and her quick response was

"I cannot tell you yet." Leslie did inform me she did not like to fly, and I could see her tension build as we taxied toward the runway.

A short wait to takeoff, and we were airborne. I could see the hospital where my wife would soon be heading to work. The complex was only a couple of years old and looked larger from the air than on the ground.

I asked Leslie a couple of questions and found her answers were just headshakes. She had a death grip on the armrest of the seat and really was in no mood to talk right now. I thought this a little unusual for a woman to go through so much fear when she could have just as easily driven. With her husband being a pilot, I should think she would have gotten over the fear of flying a long time ago.

All I could see through the window were the snow-covered Rocky Mountains below us. They had gotten quite a bit of snow the past few weeks, and everyone hoped the drought that had lasted the past few years was over. Water is the lifeblood of this state, and the more water, the better.

We had headed northwest from the airport for about twenty minutes and then tuned south. The hum of the engines put me to sleep about thirty minutes into the flight. I normally can't sleep on a plane, but the short interrupted night caught up with me.

We started to descend when I was awakened by a strange sound. It was Leslie trying to talk to wake me up, but the sound coming from her was not her normal voice. I could see the flight had taken a toll on her.

I glanced out the window and could see many of the landmarks I knew as a kid growing up in this country. I had flown into this airport many times on commercial planes and once when I was flying a round robin while in college getting solo hours logged for my private pilot's license.

I had gotten my private pilot's license and had never flown again. I liked to fly, but after college, I could never afford to rent a plane. After a few years of thinking about it, the whole idea was lost in all the hustle and bustle of just trying to survive on what you can make.

This company plane was landing in my hometown. I had left about thirty-five years ago, and since then a lot of buildings had taken place. I had been back in the area, but you don't realize how much has changed when you are in a car at ground level.

Additional reservoirs had been built and handle water for irrigation and domestic use. Many new streets filled areas that had been farmland and sage brush. It was quite odd to see areas with houses on them that weeds wouldn't grow on before. *So this is what they call progress!*

Chapter Four

The plane landed smoothly and taxied to a large hangar. The hangar was one of the largest on the tarmac, and you could put five or six planes this size in it.

As the plane came to a stop, a Cadillac pulled up, and the driver got out. After the right engine of the plane had come to a complete stop, the door was opened by Leslie's husband. He had lovingly patted her hand as he pried it off the armrest. He told her everything was all right, and it was time to depart the plane.

Leslie was the second person to get off of the plane; she was right on her husband's heels as they went down the stairs. She paused for a brief moment as if to say a short prayer that her two feet were back on the ground again, and took a couple of deep breaths to relieve some tension.

I was the next to get off and was greeted by the man who had showed up in the fancy car. He told me his name was Ambrose, and he would be my driver for the next couple of days.

As we headed to the car, I wondered how much this cost the estate, or worse yet, how much this was going to cost the estate.

Ambrose, Leslie, and I were the only people in this fancy car as we left the hangar area and headed to the main highway into town. The pilots had stayed behind to tend to the plane. I had also noticed a helicopter in the hangar when we had first arrived. I muttered to myself, *Someone around here has a bundle of money.*

Leslie acted as if she didn't hear me but was also still trying to settle back in; now she was back on the ground again. She fidgeted with her briefcase and looked at a few papers, and then she looked out the window at the Uncompahgre Plateau to the west.

The car made its way to the old-stone block courthouse. It had been there for many years, and just across the street was another stone building that was the post office. Both of these buildings were built a long time ago and were a monument to what the early small towns could afford to build in times past. Both buildings seemed smaller when I was growing up, but still had their majestic stone staircases to the entry doors.

Chapter Five

We entered through the courthouse front doors and walked to the east end of the first floor. There, we went in a door that had the name of Judge Gillipi on the glass. As we entered, we were greeted by an older woman who was sitting at the desk.

She immediately recognized Leslie and took a couple of seconds to look me over. She looked at me like I had been sent to the Principal's Office for disciplinary reasons. She then started to chat with Leslie and asked how the trip had gone, etc. Finally, Leslie got a word in and introduced me to Judge Gillipi's secretary, Janie Mae. Janie asked if we would please have a seat as it would be a few minutes before the judge would be ready.

Within a few minutes, Janie Mae emerged through the large wooden door and asked us to follow her into the office. "Sit down and make yourselves comfortable. The judge will be with you in just a moment," she added.

The judge's desk was huge and as long as a foldup table, made of solid oak and looked like it probably weighed a thousand pounds. The surface was kept neat, orderly, and everything in its own place.

I sat down and removed my cap. *Maybe I should have dressed up more for this occasion.* I had settled for a fairly new pair of black jeans and a nice shirt; no suit coats or ties for me. A suit would have to be a funeral or maybe a wedding, and I didn't think we were having either of those today. I probably couldn't fit in the slacks I have now; I hadn't worn them in a couple of years.

Leslie, on the other hand, had dressed for the occasion. I knew she had played this game before and probably many times. She was dressed in a professional suit and definitely outshined me in the clothes department.

A door behind the desk opened and a very stately elderly gentleman entered the room. He had his black robe on to make him look more official, and it was definitely doing the job. Leslie and I stood up and were quickly and sternly told to sit. The old judge may be eighty or ninety years old, and he sat himself at the desk. He had entered the room with a folder that was about three inches thick, and unlike his desk, it looked like he had just picked it up off the floor. Papers stuck out of the sides, and some were bent over on the corners and all askew.

The judge introduced himself as Ret. Judge George Gillipi. He explained he did some work for the courts since they had to cut personnel due to economic reasons. He asked if there were any questions and proceeded before anyone could have asked one, even if they wanted to.

He started by mumbling something about the final estate settlement of Christopher Smalliker. After he got started, however, he continued with all the information with a little more zest. His oratory was very clear and easily understood. He was telling a story—mine! He was telling me the story of the future and how it happens. A future should not be affected by the lack of money, property, vehicles, and whatever may come my way.

He informed me I was the only heir to this estate. There had been others whom had questioned the last will and testament, and had their day in court to challenge validity. All of this had been settled, per Christopher's request, before I had been notified of its existence. *Damn nice of him.*

The estate was called the Wheel Ranch. *Quite unique, and I'll bet that there is a Spring Creek on it too.*

There are probably at least five hundred Wheel Ranches in the western United States, and I think every county has at least one Spring Creek running in it. But I think I will take whatever comes my way, however the estate comes, as long as it does not cost me an arm and a leg.

The judge continued with his discourse about the legal description, location, financial interests, investments, stocks, bonds, and local holdings.

My mind was starting to whirl with all this information coming in all at one time and trying to keep it all straight. He was quickly losing my attention. The figures he was talking about made the forty thousand dollars Leslie had delivered to me last night seem like a drop in the ocean. He was disclosing large amounts of monies were being handled by an accountant and financial advisor from Christopher Smalliker Enterprises. He covered legal matters being handled by the law firm Leslie works for, which is also part of Christopher Smalliker Enterprises. He continued about tangible and non-tangible assets, whatever all that is.

My head was swimming with all this talk and instruction, but he just continued on. Finally, he asked if there were any questions. When I did not respond, he assured me Leslie was very competent, and she was already aware of everything he had just told us. She could answer any questions I would have, and if she couldn't, she knew where to get the answers. We signed all the necessary papers for the will to become complete and legal. The paperwork seemed like a lot to me, almost like buying a car or a house.

Chapter Six

The judge finished signing all the papers he needed to and handed them to Leslie. She thumbed through them, and every once in a while would stop and have me sign one.

As I signed the last page, Leslie let out a big sigh of relief while she gathered up and arranged all the paperwork into her briefcase. She looked as if a great weight had been lifted from her shoulders. This struck me a little odd because the whole process did not take that long, and the judge did all the reading and explaining of the forms. He directed most of the instruction toward her and not me, probably figuring I didn't know what he was talking about anyway. This seemed normal to me, and I wasn't paying that much attention after the first twenty minutes. Leslie had been working on the estate for over two years, though, so I am sure transferring everything would be a big relief, at least for today.

I had gotten bored with the whole process quite early in the reading material, as most of it made no sense to me with the legal language being used. I knew I would have a lot better idea of what was going on when I saw what had been inherited and felt very comfortable with the integrity of both the judge and Leslie. I had no doubt everything was being done to the letter, maybe more so than needed. I did recall a lot of legal land description and had lost track of the total amount of acreage, about two or three thousand acres, I believe. I heard percent of mineral, oil, and water rights; there was also something said about one-hundred-year leases on land, etc. I was ready for a walk around the block!

Finally, Leslie stood up and thanked the judge for all of his assistance and guidance on this case. I stood and also shook his hand to thank him for his assistance today. We turned and headed to the door but were interrupted by the judge. He directed his comment to me, saying, "And one cellar." He said that comment with a smile and a chuckle in his voice, and then headed out the big door he had entered through.

"What does he mean by this one-cellar statement?" I asked.

She still looked puzzled, but told me there was an old cellar on the property. It was the type of cellar built in the turn of the century to store crops for the winter without having them freeze. These cellars were very popular in the area, but most had fallen in or were dozed in over the past years. The cellar was still used as storage for old equipment and hadn't been used for years. Other than the cellar seemed in good shape, she really didn't know much more about it. She did say she really didn't know what he means by the comment.

Chapter Seven

As we were leaving the courthouse, Leslie asked if I would like to take a helicopter ride to see what I had just "signed my life away for." I agreed and watched as she opened her cell phone and quickly dialed a number. She conversed briefly and headed to the car. She told Ambrose to take me to the airport hangar after he dropped her off at her office. She had other paperwork to complete. Ambrose did as he was instructed and took her to a very new and modern building a couple of blocks away. He escorted her to the door, and I could tell he was getting additional instructions from her.

When he returned to the car, he gave out a little chuckle and stated, "She likes to be in total control or think she is anyway."

He then backed from the parking spot and headed to the main street of town.

This town had changed a lot in the last thirty years, but there was a lot that was still the same. Many of the old businesses were still there, some missing from a fire that had burned them years earlier, and some new ones that had started up.

Most of the bars were still on the Main Street and most still had the same names. All the department stores and the five-and-dime stores were long gone. If they were still in business, they had moved to the mall on the outskirts of town to try to compete with the big-box stores. I noticed one of the long-time drugstores was still on the corner it had been on when I was a kid.

Ambrose pulled the car up to the back of the hangar we had arrived at earlier in the day. The conversation had been cordial but guarded as we had passed the time of day on the way back to the airport. He exited the car and opened the door. It has been a long, long time since anyone had opened the car door for me, and the gesture took me quite by surprise.

"Are you going on the joy ride with me?" I asked.

"No," he replied. "I try to keep my feet on the ground when it comes to these things. I don't trust them as far as I can throw them."

"Will you be here when I come back?" I asked.

"Yes," he replied. "I will be with you the rest of today and tomorrow."

I walked through the door of the hangar and was met by Mr. Flemmings. He had been the copilot on the morning flight, and it now appeared he would be the pilot for this helicopter ride this afternoon. I shook his hand and asked him his name.

"John," he replied in a kind of a formal manner, which seemed strange to me for this less-than-formal atmosphere. The helicopter was a Bell Ranger and looked like the ones you see on the TV channels in Denver. The chopper was spotless and had a couple of bright red stripes on the sides. If my mind was right, the stripes were the same red color that was on the King Air airplane this morning. The people who owned these and the pilots took excellent care of them and were proud of them.

John began the trip by making sure I was buckled in right and explained the headset and how it works for communication while we are in the air. He started the chopper and after a couple of minutes, we were off. My last ride in a chopper had been a couple of years ago and took a couple of minutes to get used to it.

We headed south, and I could see the range of mountains. They were very majestic and stood out like a gem. These are the San Juan Mountains, and in my opinion, the prettiest range of mountains I have ever seen. We flew on past some high-power transmission lines and a few miles farther, we turned to the east. Below, I could see a large long paved driveway that led up to a house and outbuildings.

John interrupted my starting to let me know we were over the Wheel Ranch, and this was the lower part of the property. He told me we were coming up on the main house now, and he went into slow flight so I could get a good look. I looked at the log-style home that had been built in the style you would probably see at a national park; it was one-story high and quite large from what I could see from above. We turned to the right and flew until we came to a fence. At that point, we turned again to the left and slowly but constantly gained altitude to stay above the ground. As we flew, the terrain became slightly rougher, and the vegetation continued to change—pastures and fields yielded to juniper trees, then quaking aspen, and on to spruce trees. The land below appeared to be good grazing land with large parks between the groves of trees. We finally crested the hill and turned to the left to continue following the fence line.

We flew for a couple of miles until we came upon another fence and headed down the hillside. Part of the way down, we came to a large reservoir, and I could see another a short distance away. A stream connected the two and would get my attention in a month or so to see if there were any fish in it. The main reservoir still had ice on the surface, and there was quite a little snow to melt and go into the reservoir.

As we continued back down, I could see the house, and it looked a lot bigger from this angle. As we approached, I could see corrals and metal buildings that appeared to be for equipment storage, grain storage and lo and behold, a cellar! *Well, the judge knew something of the place.* There appeared to be a lot of machinery parked around, and most of it was pretty old, the type of worn-out and broken equipment that turns to junk.

I noticed another log house south of the main house. The cabin-style house was not as large and built in the same style. There were a couple of smaller outbuildings around it.

We continued toward the highway we had crossed on the way here and back to the airport. I asked John if he knew how many acres were there, and he told me my best bet was to ask Leslie. I continued to notice the lack of information that these people would give me themselves, always referring me to Leslie, but I felt they could tell me all I wanted to know if they felt comfortable with me. *That will come.*

We continued the flight back to the hangar on the same path as we had come out—more to see and absorb, a lot I missed on the way out. I made the comment that Leslie's office seemed to keep the flying business busy. I asked the pilot if he was the owner or part-owner of the flying service or just employed by them. He told me he contracted to fly for the company as did the other pilot. They both had been with the company for quite a few years, and Christopher kept them busy before. He said he was paid well and was covered by all the insurances and retirement programs. Both of them did the minor and daily upkeep of the planes, and the rest of the maintenance was done over at Denver.

As we approached the hangar, I could see Ambrose was still there waiting. We landed and when the blades ceased to turn, John allowed me to exit. I thanked him for the ride and told him I was sure it would not be the last joyride over the new acquisition. He finally smiled and said, "Anytime."

I walked toward Ambrose, and he greeted me with a smile. We walked through the hangar and exited through the small door on the rear of the building. The hangar was large and inside sat the King Air we had arrived in, all shiny and clean. There was also a place for the chopper next to it, but the rest, over half, was empty and completely spotless. I thought maybe I had walked into an operating room or something. I had never seen a building so clean.

I asked Ambrose if he had the time. I hadn't carried a watch in the last twelve years. He replied that it was eleven forty. I thanked him and asked, "On the back to town, is there a good place to get a little lunch? My breakfast is long gone."

Ambrose replied, "Leslie is handling that. I will see if it is ready."

He pulled out his cell phone and called her. He had her number on quick dial, and it didn't take long to get a reply. A fairly short conversation occurred, and he closed his phone.

"Lunch is ready whenever we get you there and you are ready."

"It has been a very busy morning, and I am ready now," I replied.

Ambrose chuckled as we headed to the car.

"Mind if I ride up front with you?" I asked.

"It's your car," he said. "You can ride anywhere you wish."

My car! The Cadillac was a lot fancier car than I had ever owned or even ridden in before today. Then I had a fleeting thought, *Maybe getting chauffeured around all the time is normal. Surely not!*

Chapter Eight

Arriving back at the building where we had left Leslie earlier in the day, Ambrose got out and came around to open my door. I had already opened the door and was getting out. He appeared a little disappointed he hadn't gotten the door for me, so I made a mental note to myself, *Let him open the car door. That is his job.*

Leslie was waiting inside the front door and opened it. As I entered the building, I noticed a title on the building. It read "Christopher Smalliker Enterprise Building." Below the main name, there was a list of all the offices housed in it and what floor they were on. The professional names belonged to doctors, lawyers, accountants, clinics, and dentists. *This is quite a building.*

I was escorted down the hall to an elevator with the word "private" on the door. There were no buttons to push, but as we approached, Leslie touched a control that looked like a garage door opener, and then she handed it to me.

"If you forget it, you can use the regular elevator," she said.

I thought that a little strange, but this whole day had not been what I would call normal anyway. We exited the elevator at the only stop it had a button for, and I found myself in a huge office with a large desk and a very comfortable-looking office chair behind it. The room would be easily forty square feet. There were shelves full of books and nice pictures on the walls where the room permitted.

"This is your office," Leslie informed me, and pulled out the chair as if she was a servant.

"What in the hell do I need an office for?" I asked in dismay.

"To run Christopher Smalliker Enterprises," she replied with a smirk and a smile. "Actually, the conglomerate runs itself, and you will probably use this office sparingly after a few weeks."

I thought I was just having a really wild dream, and it may be time to wake up. I continued to quiz Leslie as to some of this enterprise business I had just learned about. She explained when Christopher Smalliker had come to this area, he had accumulated a large fortune from his construction business. Almost all the upper management people worked for him before coming here, moved with him, and still work for the company.

Over the years, they had invested along with Christopher and now do a lot of the work for charity rather than business. The business had been set up to be self-sufficient and to operate very smoothly. Each department has its expertise and also keeps the welfare of the company as top priority. They have some of the best people available to keep this machine in tip-top shape. The company owns the airplanes, the King Air, the Bell, and a Learjet that is in Denver getting its inspections and minor repair. All the employees have the option to use the company's investment services, and they watch their investments closely to make the most of it. All employees have one of the best benefit packages available in the country.

I asked how the recent downturn in the economy had affected their portfolios, and she responded that their investment department had seen it coming and protected the investments with other options. The fall in the market had not affected their investments hardly at all. *Very lucky people. I am sure I am one of them.*

"How many employees are there in the company?" I asked.

"Almost one hundred," she replied. "Most of them work for the enterprise. Over the years, we have brought some of the best doctors, dentists, and other professionals, both in health as well as in other professions, to keep our employees and the local community well covered with whatever services they need, when they need it. We also have agreements with well-renowned health facilities if we cannot handle the injury or illness here."

We were interrupted by a young woman who told Leslie that lunch was ready to be served. *This place is kind of strange, but pretty damned efficient and self-sufficient.*

I took a few minutes to clean up and got my final instructions from Leslie before entering the next room. "You will be meeting the six heads of the departments. They answer to you if you want, but are very good at what they do," she said.

We stepped into a room that in my mind must have been the boardroom. People were standing around in three-piece suits, just waiting for me and lunch. Most of them looked as if they had just come from a theater presentation or were going to one. They lined up in a neat line, and I was introduced to everyone and their responsible department. I shook hands with each one. I did notice there were only five until I got to the end of the line, and Leslie stepped into her place. She reiterated her name and said she was responsible for the Legal Department. All members were very friendly and briefly explained their department. Each made sense to me, such as Investing, Security, Charity, Health Management, Accounting, Future Endeavors, and Legal. By the look in their eyes, they liked what they did very much, and they were not at all surprised by me. Somehow I felt that they pretty well knew all about me.

Leslie stated that lunch was ready, and we went and sat at some tables at the far end of the room. The lunch appeared to be a catered affair and was very wholesome and healthy foods. There were cold cuts of all types as well as hot dishes that would cater to even the pickiest eater.

All seemed content to just eat and weren't too interested in getting my first impression on the day. The talk was just table talk and a question or two that had to do with business, but there was not even much discussion. After lunch, Leslie took control of the meeting and explained most of what had gone on during the morning to the department heads. They asked a few questions that she answered, and then the meeting was over. Each shook my hand and had a quick cordial comment, and then left through doors in the wall that you couldn't even tell were there. The doors seemed to have a motion sensor, or maybe each of them had a remote. *Who knows!*

Leslie asked if I would return to my office and have a seat at the desk. I did as I was asked. She had another envelope for me and asked that I open the envelope, read it, and sign the papers if I agreed to them.

"They are very important," she commented.

As I opened the envelope and pulled the papers out, I noticed that it said Last Will and Testament. I thought I had signed all that business this morning, but as I read, I realized this will was mine. If I were to die in the next few minutes, everything I had just inherited would move on in an orderly manner to my wife and kids.

"I had better not let them know this," I joked to Leslie.

Judging from what I had already seen, every cent of my estate would be accounted for and handled in a timely and efficient manner. I sat and looked the paperwork over at this oversized desk and in this very comfortable chair. I signed the paperwork and handed it back to Leslie. She checked to see if I had signed in all the right places and thanked me. She then handed me another envelope with my name written on it. This writing was different from the rest of them. She said there was no hurry on the second one. She also said she would give me a little time alone with it.

About five minutes in this chair after lunch would put me in Neverland for about an hour, and it really only took maybe one or two. I was asleep about thirty minutes or so when I was interrupted by a buzzing noise coming from the phone. Trying to gather my senses, I grabbed for the phone and was met by Leslie's voice asking me if I would be ready to go to the property in about fifteen minutes.

I said, "That's fine with me."

I opened the envelope, and there was a piece of paper suggesting that before I go any further, I should make sure that I was alone. It stated that all these people were completely trustworthy, but what was contained in this envelope was information only for me. Inside the second envelope was a small piece of paper with a combination written on it and the location of the safe. *There must really be something of great value in the safe.*

I opened the safe and found a couple of medium-sized notepads and a spiral notebook inside a sealed envelope. Inside the spiral notebook was some information that would change my mind about a lot of things, and maybe warp it a little, but definitely change my mind as to what I had seen from the helicopter earlier. I sat back in the chair and looked around this beautiful but masculine office, wondering what I was in for. After gazing around for a few seconds, I returned to reading the spiral notebook. I realized I had inherited many more things than the judge had read about this morning, and the judge knew more about this part of the estate than he let on. I closed the safe and put the pads and notebook where they would be ready to take with me when we left.

Chapter Nine

Leslie entered the room and said it was time for us to leave. I took a ride down the elevator and outside to where Ambrose was waiting with the car. He opened the doors and let us in, and then we were off to the property. We headed south out of town and drove for about fifteen to twenty minutes. Leslie looked out the window and looked as if she was seeing it for the first time. The conversation was just small talk that did not amount to anything. I think the events of the last couple of days had taken a toll on her. We came to a large entrance made out of logs. Upon the top cross member log was a hanging wooden wagon wheel, and below it was a sign with the words Wheel Ranch burned into it. There was heavy metal gate across the entrance, stout enough you couldn't drive a tank through it. Ambrose pulled up to a keypad switch on a pole and entered the code. He told me the code, so if I needed it in the future, I would have it. The gate slowly lowered into the ground below the gate to become part of the cattle guard.

"That's quiet ingenious," I said. "How long has that been there?"

"Forever" was Ambrose's response.

We continued into the entrance, and the drive turned into a very nice and smooth road with very little loose gravel on it. The gravel only lasted for about one hundred feet and then turned to a smooth paved three-lane-wide driveway. I was amazed at how smooth the driveway was but confused why they did not pave it all the way. Upon asking that question, Leslie told me there had been some old law that said if a driveway was a certain length and was paved all the way, the county could class it as part of the county road system. The gravel section was sufficient to keep it from being annexed. *Now I know why there is a legal department for this company.* This smooth road continued all the way up to the main house.

"I don't know how anyone that doesn't do this for a living can keep up with all the intricate details," I said.

"We have researched all the laws on the books for the county and state to make sure all the properties are in compliance," she said. "That's why we are here."

We approached the house, and I noticed a large grassy yard area. The house was larger than it looked from the air. We pulled up to the front porch and waited for Ambrose to open the car doors. The front porch was enclosed with a screen to keep the bugs out. The exterior of the house was of log construction and looked like it could withstand a direct bomb blast. The logs were smooth finished, and the chinking between was straight and even as far as you could see. A lot of care had been taken when this was built. We entered the porch and were greeted by an area full of old, solid built, and comfortable-looking patio furniture. There were a couple of rockers, lounges, regular chairs, and a lot of end tables. I knew this was patio furniture, but it looked good enough to fit in the front room. All of this furniture was probably fifty years old. This front porch had a very friendly feeling and would greet many visitors and make them feel right at home. This space would be a nice area to sit and read a book, have a beer, or just enjoy the sunset.

The front door was two inches thick and looked as if a car couldn't crash through it. It was very well balanced and could be opened without any effort at all. The entry opened into a large mudroom where a lot of coats and boots could be left without stacking them up. Then the entryway opened into a spacious room with couches, chairs, occasional tables, end tables, and a large native stone fireplace. There were a lot of lamps mixed in with the furniture and some very expensive-looking rugs on the hardwood floor. You could almost see yourself in the shine off the floor. This room was easily two or three thousand square feet in area. All the furniture was masculine looking, but had a hint of exquisite hidden in. No expense had been spared when this was purchased. Although large, the room had a warm feeling to it and was pleasant to just stand and look at.

We progressed to the next room, which was the dining room. It was also almost as big. It had a large wooden table that would easily seat twenty people. Around the edges were additional tables and chairs that would accommodate another twenty or so people. There were built-in china hutches full of glassware of all different sizes and shapes, but enough to set every available space. I was sure my wife would be able to inform me of their worth, but as with everything I had seen up to this point, it was all fine quality.

We went into a very impressive kitchen. There were a lot of copper pots and pans hanging from racks mounted on the ceiling, and all of them shined as if new. There was a gas stove that looked large enough to cook a major meal for thirty to forty people at one time. It had a massive hood over it with a large notation on a sign about the fire suppression system that could be used if needed. The entire kitchen area appeared as if it were designed for a restaurant, but at one end, it sat a regular-sized stove, refrigerator, microwave, and a horseshoe-shaped counter where everyone could sit around and talk while meals are being prepared. A pantry was off to the side of the kitchen; it had an efficient amount of shelves. I figured in my head quickly, and came to a figure of five or six thousand dollars of food to fill this up. At the present time, it appeared to have plenty of food stored there.

Down a hallway from the kitchen and the dining room were two oversized restrooms the guests could use if needed. Farther down the hall were six extra big bedrooms, each with its own attached full bathroom. A king-size bed, a large walk-in closet, dressers, a vanity where a woman could put the finishing touches on her makeup, a couple of large easy chairs, a couple of small tables with lamps on them and one larger table with four chairs, maybe for playing cards, rounded out the room. Each room also had an entrance to a private porch area and had a screen on the outside wall. These bedrooms were more like an apartment than a bedroom.

Back towards the front part of the house was the library with shelves filled with books from the floor to the ceiling. There was the old-style ladder that was hooked to the wall, and you roll it to the section you wanted and climb the ladder, if needed, to reach the upper shelves. A couple of overstuffed chairs and some tables were strategically placed around; there were lamps to aid in getting enough light. At one end, there was a desk with a large computer screen. At the far end, there was a single door I soon found out went to an office. This one appeared to be identical to the one in town, except it was not as expansive. All the furniture was the same design, and the chair behind the desk looked to be as comfortable as the one in town. The office appeared to have everything needed to converse with anyone in the world if needed.

"This is quite a house," I commented. "When was it built?"

"In the early fifties," she replied, "but it has been updated a couple of times."

"It didn't quite look this large from the air," I said.

"There is a full basement underneath," she replied. "It houses all the utilities, a recreation area, and a workout area."

Having seen almost all the upstairs, we headed down the wide staircase to the basement. The room open up into a recreation area with pool tables, a Ping-Pong table, arcade games—both old and new—and a couple of game tables that were set and looked as if they were ready for a fun night of gambling. On one side of the room was a bar area about twelve feet long and a beautiful mirror behind the bar. There appeared to be every kind of booze, all in different shapes and colored bottles. There were glasses of different shapes and sizes for specific drinks. I am sure I would have no idea what glass went with which drink. A good bartender could quite keep a crowd happy with this setup. Behind the bar were refrigerated areas with different kinds of labeled beers.

The large fireplace on the outside wall was constructed the same as the fireplace upstairs. The other side of the basement was split into two rooms. One was a home theater with a huge screen and about thirty theater-style overstuffed chairs. I was sure the setup had the most recent, or a couple of years old, surround sound available.

Next to this room was a workout room with a wide assortment of different machines to work your butt off if you wanted. There were a couple of TV screens in here, so you wouldn't get lonely if you were working out by yourself. There were also mats on the floor and a basketball hoop at one end.

"You would never have to set a foot outside around here," I commented.

Leslie told me the utilities were located through the door at the end of the room. She really didn't say much about them, probably because she didn't know about them or figured I could figure that out for myself.

Back upstairs, we exited a side glass door that took us to the patio. There were very nice chairs and tables set around on the stained concrete patio. The concrete had a tile look, and if you really didn't know better, you would think it was tile. There was a large brick barbeque assembly at one end with a stainless steel grill in it. The whole area looked as if it were ready for a party. On one end were a hot tub and a sauna area. I could tell they had been built a few years earlier because of the style, but I was also sure they would work with a flick of a switch. Everything in this area had been planned for the pleasure of the homeowner and their guests and was convenient and as pleasurable as possible.

The large backyard was landscaped tastefully but a little plain. There were deciduous trees and bushes. It did lack a lot of beds for flowers and plants. As we walked around the south side of the yard, I spotted a large greenhouse located just off of the patio area. Leslie explained Christopher had grown his own vegetables all year round, and the greenhouse was set up to sustain that growth.

"How many people work around here?" I asked. "I mean, like gardeners and people to mow and clean, etc."

"Christopher had about twelve household people working here, which includes the maids, cooks, gardeners, and general laborers," she replied. "Christopher was not the kind of person to work in the soil. The last couple of years he did cut back on the outside help and let it take care of itself. We did have a few workers here to just maintain the grounds waiting for the final settlement."

We returned to the house, and Leslie went to find Ambrose. As she returned, she asked, "If you would like to spend the night here, I have had the maid ready a room for you. We brought some of the food from lunch, and it is in the refrigerator if you want."

"That would be great with me," I replied.

I went into the office and was seated at the desk in the very comfortable chair. I deposited the notepads I had been carrying around since we had left the office. I put them in a drawer and closed it before Leslie returned.

Ambrose suggested we just look around the farmyard for now and check out the rest of the place tomorrow when there would be more time. I agreed, and we left the main house for the first of many tours of this place full of surprises.

Chapter Ten

We headed toward the machinery sheds and passed by what I thought was a grain storage bin when I had flown over in the chopper. Ambrose informed me the building is an observatory, and you sit in a chair and dial in what you want to see in the sky. A computer control then puts the telescope in the correct position, and you look out into the night sky in all its wonder. The computer automatically keeps track of the object by continuously adjusting the telescope for the movement of the earth.

"This sounds a little extravagant to me," I said, "at least for a farmhouse."

"Only the best" was his reply.

"Between greenhouses, gardens, and an observatory, my wife will be in seventh heaven," I told him.

We walked to the farm shop. It looked like a typical farm shop area with a piece of farm equipment sitting here and there. We stepped inside the walkthrough door, and he turned on the light. Inside was spotless and very well organized. The inside was not what I would call a typical farm shop; however, the floor was concrete and painted a shiny gray. Along one side of the shop was a floor hoist for lifting cars and light trucks. Large red toolboxes formed a line along the wall, and a quick count came to six. Each drawer on each box had a sticker or stickers on the drawer handle telling you what was located within each drawer. I pulled a drawer out that said Sockets, and there were sockets in standard sizes, from one quarter to four-inch size. This drawer had to weigh three to four hundred pounds, but it pulled open easier than a kitchen drawer. We walked farther into the shop, and I could see test equipment, not as much as for the real new cars but for the cars from maybe thirty-five to forty-five years ago, like the late sixties and early seventies, cars that ran without computers as we know them today.

Farther along the shop wall was an area for welding and fabricating metal objects. Along the other side of the shop wall was mostly storage area of bolt bins and neatly stacked shelves full of stuff. The workbenches were heavily built to withstand long years of service. The shop area had a heat exchanger type of heat system in the ceiling. I had never seen anything quite like them, but was sure that the heat source was located in some other building or outside. I knew I would be spending a lot of time in this area working on a couple of projects that I had wanted to start for a long time. My 1967 Dodge pickup was one that just popped into my mind.

As we left the shop, Ambrose turned off the lights and closed the doors.

"Do you lock this place up at night?" I asked.

"It does it itself and will let you know if a door is not closed and locked. I'll show you how the system works when we get back to the house."

We continued to the next building and entered through a small side door. It was the machinery storage area. There were tractors, hay balers, windrowers, plows, discs, a small combine, corn choppers, and other miscellaneous implements. All were arranged in a very tight and neat manner, and they all looked as if they were brand new.

"Who takes care of all the equipment?" I asked.

He blushed a little and said, "I do."

"Do you do all of the maintenance on them too?"

"No, they bring in mechanics from town or send them to town to have them serviced and repaired" was his reply. "I just wash them and keep them here to protect them from the weather. We haven't done much with them the past couple of years. The whole place had been let go since Christopher got real sick and died. I run the tractor engines once a month to exercise them and try to keep the seals lubricated and the batteries charged up."

"I am very pleased," I said. "You have done an excellent job. They all look as if they are new."

"Thanks," he replied. I could see his pride swell in his eyes.

We continued the walk through the machine shed, and I was amazed at just how much equipment was stored in this space. To get the equipment stacked in so tight and straight must have taken quite a long time.

"Do you do the farming?"

"No," he replied. "There was a man and his sons who took care of the place. I just kept the stuff clean. About a month after Christopher found out he was ill, the man and his sons were all killed in a car wreck in Arizona. Since then, nothing has been done here. We couldn't find anyone who knew or wanted to take on the responsibility to keep this place up. We had a few applicants, but they did not know anything about farming. After a while, Christopher gave up looking and said the next owner would know how to handle what needed to be done."

It is apparent the income from the farm wasn't needed to keep it going; this is going to keep me busy for a while.

We left the machinery shed and walked past a grain bin. It was quite large and was also set up to dry the grain if needed. It had an auger coming out of the bottom and another one that headed toward the corrals. We walked past the corrals, and I could tell they hadn't been used for years.

"Did Christopher raise any livestock here?" I asked.

"No, he didn't," he replied. "I don't really know when the last time these corrals and animal sheds have been used. It has to be before Christopher bought the place in the late eighties."

"That is a shame. These are quite nice sheds and corrals for animals. Even though they haven't been used for years, they are in pretty good shape. A few sheep or cows could really live it up around here," I commented. "Since it is getting late in the afternoon, let's take in the cellar and then call it a day."

Ambrose looked at me in kind of a strange way and then commented, "You really don't know what you ask, but okay."

We went to the cellar and went inside the small entry door. Ambrose turned on the lights, and I soon realized this was no ordinary cellar. This appeared to be a very large Quonset hut that had been dug into the ground a little to make it appear that it was an old-style cellar. Along the sides were areas fenced off to keep what was stored there from falling out. Stored items appeared to be more equipment and many pieces of horse-drawn equipment that looked as if it had been there for fifty years. On the floor, there was a large metal plate about fifty foot long and thirty feet wide. Ambrose pushed a large green button on a control panel, and this metal floor began to slowly lower. The plate tipped down on one end to make a ramp into the area below, enough that I believe you could back an enclosed semitrailer into it without any problem. When Ambrose pushed the button, there had been a loud humming noise, similar to the sound of a large electric motor energizing. I assumed the noise was the sound of hydraulic jacks lowering the floor ramp. When the floor stopped, we walked down the ramp to the floor below. I walked down this ramp with the great anticipation of what was hidden under the first floor. At the bottom of the ramp was an enormous round area large enough to store that semitruck if one ever went down here. There appeared to be six large steel doors around the perimeter of the room, each with a different color dot painted on it. The room was well lit and totally constructed of concrete, quite a large project for a farm.

"Where do these go?" I asked.

"Only a couple work" was Ambrose's reply.

He walked to the door with the green dot and turned a lever next to the door. The door began to roll open, and the lights simultaneously came on inside the area behind the door. I walked to the door and felt like I had fallen back in forty years' time. There in front of me was a very huge room full of vintage automobiles from the sixties and early seventies. They all appeared as if they had just come off the showroom floor, and many of them had the dealer stickers still in the windows. The first to really catch my eye was a forest-green 1969 Dodge Charger with a black vinyl roof. As I approached this car, it appeared to have all the whistles and bells that were available when the model was new. The notation on the side of car said Hemi, the biggest engine Chrysler Corporation put in these cars. Chrysler, also known as Mopar, was known for big powerful engines in its vehicles. A further look around brought a lot of Mopar cars, like Cudas, Road Runners, Challengers, and a multitude of others. There were also GM and Ford muscle cars, but not to the extent of the Mopar products. At the start of the row of cars on the right side was a 1974 Dodge Ramcharger, which looked exactly like the one I was driving when I had helped Christopher so long ago. It was the burnt orange color that was so popular that year. It had a white top and the large chrome wheel covers, they were stock. The one I had owned was a very good vehicle to me at the time, and this one brought back a lot of fond memories.

I walked to the Ramcharger and opened the door. This vehicle was spotless and even smelled as if it were a brand new unit. I sat in the seat and looked down and noticed the keys were in it.

"Can I start it?" I asked.

"Sure," he replied

I turned the key, and the old familiar Chrysler starter whine engaged. The unit started right off as if I had just shut it off. I let the engine run for a couple of minutes then turned the switch off.

"I suppose you start all of these once a month to keep them exercised too," I said to him.

"More often than that," he replied. "Gets pretty noisy in here though. There is a ventilation system that completely changes the air inside here every three minutes. We also have a system that pulls the vapors off of the exhaust as they run."

"This place would make any car enthusiast go crazy." I replied. "I don't remember any of this being discussed or on the list that the judge read this morning."

"This is what they consider minor miscellaneous" was his reply. "There will be quite a bit of that stuff."

I walked toward the entry door and almost drooled all over myself as I walked past all the cars. A semi-quick calculation on the worth of the contents of this tunnel-shaped room was well over five million. I had seen a "Cuda" identical to one of these on sale on TV for over a million by itself. *Minor miscellaneous!*

There were other doors with the painted dots on them, so we headed to the next in line. The first door came to a close and locked the second, which started to open via the lever next to it, just like the first one. The room also was built in the tunnel style and had the look of a large industrial plant.

"This is the utility area for the property. You pay no utility bills at all to keep this place running, and you never will have to. The electricity is produced on the property with a hydroelectric generator fed from the upper reservoir you saw when you were on your flight this morning. Spring Creek is the name of the waterway that is used, but it is all man-made. Mother Nature provides the water, and the rest is handled here."

I was taken aback a little to think that this idea wasn't anything new. I knew this technology was around a long time but not used very often. Whoever built this property was looking to make as little footprint as possible.

"The water treatment system is also in this room, and it utilizes a double osmosis system to clean and purify the water. It does not put chlorine or chemicals in the water. This water system was developed in the late forties and works as well as anything invented since. Oh, I shouldn't have said that!" he said.

"Why not?" I asked.

"Some of this stuff is supposed to be classified and real confidential. No one is supposed to find out about a lot of this stuff" was his quick reply. "Christopher will explain all of this on a disc he made."

Ambrose went to a control panel and opened it. Inside was a DVD disc sealed in a box.

"Christopher asked me to give this to only you. It will explain a lot of the things that are located here and why they are here. A lot of the things I don't even know about and don't really want to know. Some of them you will think are one thing, but are really something else entirely. It will also introduce you to Christopher again and the Wheel Ranch. Leslie doesn't know about most of this stuff, and she is really quite thorough with her job. It would probably be better if it stays that way for a while anyway."

Ambrose paused for a while and then continued. "It will explain the paved driveway is also a drag strip with the Christmas Tree and everything. He tells you how to make it operate, and that way you can see just how well all those cars run and perform."

"There is a regular drag strip Christmas Tree at the driveway for starting drag races?" I inquired.

"Yes" was his only reply.

I could tell by the look in his eye and tone in his voice that the cars were his pride and joy, and even though they belonged to me, he would keep them polished and running well.

I looked at the DVD and noticed it was sealed very securely. It had some type of heat wrap around it, and I knew I would have to break the box to get it out. That's nothing new; I usually have to break the boxes anyway to get the discs out.

I put the case in my coat pocket, and Ambrose closed the second door. We exited the cellar basement and watched as the light shut off, and the big ramp door closed back to floor level.

"This is quite a place," I commented. He nodded in agreement.

Not anybody I know has a drag strip for a driveway. *Some of the people who lived here had quite an imagination.* We entered the yard and walked toward the house. I noticed all of a sudden it looked about twice as big as it was before. Amazing how things change from a different angle.

Chapter Eleven

Leslie was in the kitchen as we entered the house.

"I made sure there was coffee, coffeemaker, sugar and cream available for you in the morning," she said. "The old housekeeper lives in town and was out to make it comfortable for you to stay. We gave her a small list of your likes as far as breakfast and your coffee. We brought leftovers from lunch, or if you want to go to town for supper, we can do that also."

I agreed leftovers sounded fine to me. It was beginning to be a very long day, and another trip to town and back did not sound good at all.

"I will have a little something later and probably be in bed by nine," I replied.

"If there is nothing else, I think we will head to town for the night," Leslie said. "Ambrose will be out about eight in the morning."

"He said something about locking the buildings and showing me how to do that," I said.

He took me to the office and opened a panel you couldn't notice was even there.

"Just push the lock button when you want all of it to lock up. It even locks the gate on the drive if you want. The car has an override, so I can open it in the morning on my way in."

"Sounds good to me," I responded. I then watched them get into the car and go toward the gate. They got onto the highway and headed north into town. Finally, I could see them no more but just stood and looked at the splendor I could see from the front of this house. Whoever picked this spot had a very good eye for the beauty of Mother Nature.

I went back inside after a few minutes and went to the office. I sat down in the second comfortable chair of the day and realized that the same man owned them both—me! I looked at the desk clock and saw that it was just five o'clock. I thought I would give my wife a few more minutes to get home and get the animals settled. I decided to see what was in each of the desk drawers and how many pencils, pens, and anything else were left behind. All the drawers were very neat, and there sat the envelope I had brought from town, just as I had left it. I finally decided enough time had gone past and dialed the home phone number. *I hope she is sitting down for this.*

My wife picked up the phone on the second ring, and we passed the cordial business of the day and how her day had gone. Finally, I asked her if she was ready for this; I hoped she was sitting down. I told her all about the day, except specifics, and just glazed over the whole inheritance information. I told her I would be home tomorrow night and explain this whole thing as I understood it. I did tell her she could give them her resignation in the morning when she went to work.

"I think I will wait until I see all of this" was her reply.

I told her about the greenhouse, rose garden, and observatory.

"I think you are making all of this up!" she said.

I told her she would just have to see it for herself. She asked a few questions, and then we decided we had talked enough. I glanced at the clock and noticed we had been on the phone for almost forty-five minutes. That is more than I usually talk on the phone in a month.

"You have a safe trip home tomorrow. Don't get lost wandering around that place" was her parting response.

After the phone call, I decided to take a slow walk back through the house to see what I had missed the first time through. The trip through earlier had been a quick one, and now I had nowhere to go for the rest of the night.

I went to the kitchen and checked to see what food the housekeeper had brought me from lunch. There appeared to be some of everything that was laid out at lunch, and it was all neatly laid out in the refrigerator. There was also enough for me to eat for about a week. I realized I wasn't ready for food yet and decided a nice highball would be great right now. I made my way through the house and found the bar. I stood looking at all the different liquors that were represented here and decided there must be at least one of everything made in the world. Most of this stuff I had never heard of and would not have the least idea on what to do with it except drink it. I found a bottle of my normal whiskey and poured a drink in one of the bar glasses. Turning around from the bar, I remembered the DVD

Ambrose had left me and realized it was still in my coat pocket. I returned to the office where my coat was flung over a chair and retrieved the DVD.

While walking through the house, I noticed it was very quiet. There were no appliances running or clocks ticking or anything making any noise. In a way, it was quite pleasant after the crazy day but amazing that it could be that quiet. We now live within a half mile of a railroad track, and there was a busy county road in front of the house; there always seemed to be background noise.

Chapter Twelve

I went into the room with the TV and figured out how everything I needed to watch this DVD worked. I found the remote and picked a seat to sit in for the show. The DVD started, and the face that appeared on the screen was of a man who looked as if he had been ill for quite a while. He introduced himself as Christopher Smalliker and thanked me again for the forty-dollar loan a long time ago and the roadside help I had given him.

As I watched the program, I realized I had seen this man within the past few years. Where I lived, there had been a house for rent three or four summers ago, and there was just a plywood sign hung between two fence posts to advertise. On a Saturday, the man on the screen had stopped to ask about the particulars of the place for rent. We had talked for about thirty minutes about all kinds of things. He finally said he would think about the rental and left. I knew now he must have just been checking on me. Oh well, on with the show.

Christopher Smalliker gave me a quick explanation of his life and where I had fit in. He had been orphaned when he was eighteen, because his parents had been killed in an automobile accident. When our paths first crossed, he was going to Nevada for a job interview with an old friend of his father's. He had gotten the job and worked for a construction company that specializes in doing secret jobs for the U.S. government of all types. He worked for the company for ten years, and had the opportunity to purchase the company because the owner wanted to retire.

Christopher Smalliker Enterprises started out and continued to do the same type of work as before. He surrounded himself with people he could trust fully and thus made the business as I saw it in town—six departments to take care of themselves, the company and its assets. The company continued the construction work for the government until late 1998. Christopher had accumulated a large sum of money and bought the Wheel Ranch. He sold the construction company but retained the name, because by now it had built such a good reputation in the communities and states where he had worked.

Christopher had brought the infrastructure of his business with him, and it continues to grow today. He bought the ranch because of what was underground and not so much of what was on top. He had heard about the property from the former boss who had built this in the very early fifties. The program continued by saying he would come back to what was underground at a later time.

He continued the story of his life. In 2006, he was diagnosed with a terminal illness that even with all of his money he could not beat. He tried for six months to find any cure or anything possible and spent money like there was no end. Finally, he came to the conclusion that there was no beating it and decided to do as much good as he could with his money.

He had kept tabs on me over the years. He was going to pay me back for the money I had given him so he could get to the job interview. He stated he just never quite got around to getting it done. He decided to give me his estate instead. With the Security Department of his company and ties to the government over the years, he had all the vital information on me and all of my family. He could tell me where I was and what I was doing almost any time in the past thirty eight years. This Big Brother idea didn't sit too well with me; for someone to be able to tell you what you had in the bank or what you owed the world was none of anyone's business, but it was a little late now.

When he got ill, he researched all of my habits, my likes and dislikes, hobbies, etc., to make sure I would take this place, with all its oddities, and continue on with his ideas and functions for the next couple of generations. He did not want it sold off for development to just anyone. Through all the information they found on me, Christopher concluded I was the right person to keep this place going.

Chapter Thirteen

To tell me all about this place, Christopher started by telling me that no one alive knows all there is to know about this property. He was the last. If I am watching this disc, then he has also expired. While working for the employer in Nevada, he got wind of this place and got all the blueprints and suppliers.

"The project actually started in 1948 with the acquisition of the land by the U.S. government. That was fairly easy because some of the land belonged to the government already. The plan was to build a test station here for new inventive equipment to make the everyday person's life easier. As the Cold War started to escalate and everyone was worried about the communists, the idea of this project seemed to change with the times. The test station idea was expanded to become a self-sufficient bomb shelter that could and would survive a nuclear attack. There are a lot of experimental technologies in the ground here.

"Just to back up a minute, under this ground is a complex made out of reinforced concrete that was developed in the late forties. The concrete is so strong the formula has never been released. For every two inches of concrete by this formula, it is equal to sixteen inches of regular concrete used for construction. The walls are still two feet thick at least, so you are pretty safe in there. The construction is shaped like a large wagon wheel with six spokes extending at equal degrees to the outer rim. The rim connects all the spokes and is large enough to drive a Jeep or small truck all the way around. The spokes are tunnels made in the rock and have lighting and electricity in them. They are all finished in high-powered concrete and quite pleasant to be in. No one knows about the last four tunnels, only that there are doors, and no one knows about the small tunnel around the outside of the spokes.

"All of this was constructed in the area about the time there were other large construction projects going on such as dams. There was never any suspicion raised by the project and no questions asked. All the money spent was allocated in other projects and doesn't show up anywhere.

"After the completion, there were six permanent scientists assigned here to get all the new technology assembled and set up to work properly. This is the reason for the six identical bedroom living suites and its privacy.

"Most of the technology is still here and has been operating for over sixty years. Some has been replaced, but most has stayed away from the computer age of equipment.

"You probably didn't notice there are no power lines to the property. All the electricity is produced on the property by hydroelectric generation. The two reservoirs are designed for that main use. They also furnish irrigation water for the lower farm ground. During the day or high use, the units generate electricity for use on the entire property, and at night, they pump water from the lower reservoir back to the upper reservoir. Most of the water comes from runoff from the winter, but there is an underground supply available at any time to refill the huge reservoirs to the east of here.

"The water from the house is purified and also returned to the reservoirs. There is very little or no footprint of this place to the environment. There are also some small wind generators on the property that help with the demand. At the time this was built, solar collection was too large to hide for the small amount of electricity produced. All these units have a lot of spare parts and backup systems galore, typical of government projects. The utility tunnel is crammed full of these parts and repair manuals if needed. Also, there are still government service contracts on this equipment, and this facility is serviced regularly.

"I am sure by now Ambrose has shown you the tunnel with the autos. These are my collection, and all are restored to new condition with original parts. Most are restored to showroom specs, but a few are beefed up a little to get your heart pumping. The real hard one to find was the Ramcharger. I hope you like it. These cars are Ambrose's babies, and he takes excellent care of them.

"I am sure Ambrose showed you the utility tunnel. This compound was designed to be totally self-sufficient. The house will hold six couples with two children each and have all the luxury available. As you have seen, there are plenty of storage and cooking areas in it and plenty of room for you to roam. Most of it is just a regular house, but there are some features I will tell you about later. There are additional areas for housing in the utility tunnel with complete cooking, eating, sanitary, and recreation facilities for many more people. There is also a distillery, wine press, and storage for the products of your labor if you so desire in the utility tunnel. There are cases of wine from the last forty years and a lot of small barrels of distilled treats stored down there. The label on this is of course Wheel Ranch. All the recipes are in a large book in the office in the still room."

Chapter Fourteen

The video continued. Tunnel 4 was the Noah tunnel, because there are facilities to house a lot of different animals for food and reproduction. There is a lot of storage for feeds and beddings. Four has an elaborate facility to dispose of all the waste, and it is done so no one on the outside knows it is going on. All the pens are folded up along the walls now, as there was no need to set them all up. Storing the pens opens the area up immensely. It leaves a lot of room for additional storage of farm equipment, etc. There is an elevator in the corral area to move things up and down into this tunnel. The hoist is not as large as the one in the cellar, but works well if needed. Many of these things have not been used for a few years, because there was no need to store things down there.

"Tunnels Three, Five, and Six are really secured tunnels, and the only way in is with the proper digital codes. The only person with those codes is me. I will give them to you in a book of other codes and safe combinations. All of this secrecy may seem stupid, but you have to remember why this place was built. There are a lot of good surprises in those tunnels, but I would keep most of it to myself for a while until you really get settled. A small example of it is in the safe in the library area.

"The safe is behind the books on the fifth shelf, one and a half foot from the right edge of the shelf. The combination is 25 right, 40 left, 3 right, 17 left, and then right to 9. If I were you, I would stop this CD and go to check this safe out. The contents may make the rest of this CD make more sense."

I noted the numbers and stopped the CD. I went to the library and found the books as he had directed. Behind them was a safe about eighteen square inches, built into the shelves and the wall. I used the combination, and it worked the very first time. I opened the door and a light lit inside the safe cavity. I reached in and pulled out a couple of envelopes and then a couple of bundles of money. All the money were one-hundred-dollar bills and appeared to be as least as much as Leslie had given me the night before in the lobby of the Hilton.

They must have a printing machine around here that just keeps kicking out those things, I said to myself.

In the bottom of the safe were three smaller but heavy objects. I pulled the first one out, and it appeared to be a small gold bar. I pulled the other two out and set them next to its partners. They were quite heavy but not as heavy as the ones you see in the movies where it is quite a strain to lift one of them.

There was writing on the bars and then a serial number: Bars were one, two, and three respectively. I returned the three small bricks to the safe and the bundles of money. I opened the envelopes, and after a quick glance knew these should be read after all the rest of this crazy place had been figured out, or kind of think I know what is going on. I returned everything I had taken out of the safe, closed the door, spun the combination, and returned the books to their places in the order I had taken them out. I almost felt like a thief going through the safe in this entirely empty house and learning all the secrets there were to learn.

All this newfound knowledge and the excitement of the day were starting to take its toll. As I walked back to the entertainment area of the house, I could feel myself starting to drag along. I sat down on a chair in front of the TV but did not turn it on. I sat there for about ten minutes and decided to go get something to eat as hunger was starting to set in.

I quickly made myself a sandwich from the leftovers from lunch and ate it while standing at the counter. It tasted good, but because of the late hour, I didn't eat a lot. I picked up my mess and returned everything to the refrigerator that needed to go there. I decided to step outside and get a little fresh air before turning in. I grabbed my jacket and put it on as I stepped outside the front door of the front porch. The night was a beautiful clear night, and all the stars were out in all of their glory. The moon was going to be full but was just starting to come over the horizon. It would be big, just like a great big pumpkin coming up. I stood and watched the moon's arrival and all the stars. I found a few of the constellations I knew like the Big and Little dippers to make sure they hadn't wondered off during the day.

I enjoyed the spring evening but finally gave up and decided it was time for me to get some beauty sleep. Lord knows I can use all of that I can get.

On the go all day, except for the catnaps I got, the experience of the day had been a real thrill. I was introduced to a lot of new things, become the proud owner of a beautiful place as far as I could tell, and was now figuring out I had taken a hold of a lot more than I could totally remember or think about today. I walked down the hall and went to the room that had been set up for me. I turned on the light in the bedroom and then backtracked through the house, turning off all the lights. I would hate to get lost in the dark in this house until I was used to the setup of each room.

I commented to myself as I made my turn off light trip, *You are as bad as the kids about turning off the light when you leave a room.*

I got ready for bed and climbed in.

"Rather hard," I said out loud. I noticed a control on the nightstand and concluded, "Christopher Smalliker didn't scrimp on anything. Didn't have to."

I adjusted the bed to my liking, and they turned off the light. I lay in the darkness until my eyes adjusted to the dim light. I quickly made the assessment of the location of the bathroom if needed and was out like a light.

Chapter Fifteen

The chime of the doorbell woke me, and I jumped out of bed before becoming totally awake. I looked at the clock, and it said the time was eight. I haven't slept that late in a very long time. I went to the door and opened it. There was Ambrose, all fresh and ready for another day. He gave me a quick good morning.

He entered the room and asked, "Have you made the coffee yet?"

"No," I replied. "I was really lazy and just got up."

"I'll make the coffee if you want to get ready for the day," he replied. "It will be a short day today, and your plane is scheduled for two o'clock. These pilots like to get off the Eastern Slope early on Fridays."

"Sounds good to me," I said. "I have a lot of stuff to hash over and get used to."

On my way back to my bedroom, I stopped and picked up the CD I had been watching the night before. I took a nice long shower and didn't worry about running out of hot water. Finally finished and dressed, I headed to the kitchen for a cup of coffee.

Ambrose was sitting at the counter and had just poured two cups of coffee.

"Smells good," I said as I entered.

I took one cup and added my standard cream and sugar and took a sip to make sure it had cooled off enough to drink.

"Looks like it is going to be a nice day," Ambrose said.

"Good, maybe we can explore more of the outside area today."

"Not today" was his reply. "Leslie needs you at the office to get more formality done. Also, she needs a schedule of your plans."

"Hell, I don't know what my plans are. How am I supposed to tell her?" I blurted out.

"Don't let her know, or she will have a whole list of stuff for you to do" was his reply. "She can get a little bossy at times. Do you want breakfast?"

"I'll just munch on this stuff in the refrigerator. I am not a big breakfast eater," I replied.

After I finished a quick breakfast, we walked around outside just looking at the buildings and got filled in on each function. We did a quick tour of the other house on the property, which was called the hired-help house. The help appeared to live in a nicer home than I was living in at the present time.

As we prepared to leave for town, I went back into the house to gather up my duffel bag, all the letters, and the CD I had been watching last night. I straightened up the bed so the housekeeper wouldn't think I was a total slob. I put the important things in the duffel bag. *It was kind of strange, putting important things in a duffel bag instead of a toolbox.*

We headed back to town to the office and took the private elevator up to my office. Leslie met us and introduced me to Linda.

"Linda will be your temporary secretary to help you get used to your new schedule."

"New schedule?" I asked. "I thought I was going to retire."

A new schedule sounds like someone has other plans for my time than retirement. Smalliker had done me a favor, I hoped, but these people were going to keep me busy.

Leslie requested that I have a chair at my desk, and then she started through the paper shuffle. She had many forms to fill out and sign. She explained that all of this was necessary in case of my death. All of this would make the inheritance stay as a whole instead of totally losing it to taxes and court battles. Christopher had done the same with my inheritance, so I had paid a minimum amount of tax upon the settlement of his estate. The process seemed like legal manipulation, but Leslie assured me it was for me and my family's best interest.

We continued with a lot more paperwork, and she told me most were copies from the prior day. When she was finished, and we had killed at least five or six trees, she pulled a briefcase from next to the desk and opened it up. She placed the paperwork inside and closed it. It had combination locks on the latches, and she gave me a piece of paper with the combinations.

I told her I had about three or four million questions, and I would write them down after I had read all the paperwork she had just awarded me. I am sure many of the things I was thinking about would be explained as I read through them.

I asked if there were any special days I had to return for meetings, etc. She informed me there was not, and Ambrose would continue to keep an eye on the place in the country and not to worry about it.

"Are you going to move here and make it a permanent home?" she asked.

"I am sure there is no reason not to" was my reply. "Everything I own is right here."

Chapter Sixteen

Lunch time arrived, and we went to a nice restaurant not far from the office. We had a very nice meal, but they served more than I could comfortably eat. When the bill came, Leslie just signed her name on the ticket.

"I take it we have a running account here?" I asked.

"Yes, this is one of the many businesses we own or have financial interests in over the area," she replied. "You will learn over time which is which."

"In all of this paperwork, is there a comprehensive list of all the assets we own as a company and the assets owned only by me?"

"Yes, and it will make more sense to you after you relocate here and get used to the day-to-day routine," she replied. "There is a directory for everything and your relationship to it. An example is this restaurant. We own the building, the lot, and financed the chef to get it started up. All are doing fine."

Chapter Seventeen

Time was running out, so Ambrose and I went back to the airport. The beautiful King Air was sitting outside of the hangar waiting. I thanked Ambrose for all of his help boarding the plane. The pilots were very cordial and after closing the door, we were headed to the runway. We took off without any delay and were headed north out of town. Below, I could see a farm I had worked on when I was a teenager, and appeared to look the same as it did the last time I had seen the farm. We climbed to cruise altitude, but I was asleep before they had cut their engines back for normal cruise. I awoke as we were making the final turn approaching the airport. Right now, it seemed like I had only been gone for a few wild hours instead of since yesterday morning. A very smooth landing, a short taxi to a spot on the tarmac, and the flight for me was over.

As the engines spun to a halt, the pilot exited the cabin and told me he would drive me home.

"Full service chauffer service for you today?" I asked.

"I don't get to do much of it. Usually, they have someone on the ground arranged before we land. It is a nice change from the set routine they usually have us on."

The ride was about twenty minutes, and I arrived before my wife had gotten home from work. I got out of the car and got my bag and briefcase. I thanked him for the smooth ride across the mountains. I told him to thank his partner for me. I wished him a safe flight, and he left for the airport.

I opened the back door of the house and was instantly mauled by the two dogs. They could not get enough attention and scratches behind the ears to suit them. Finally, they began to settle down and get back to normal. I took them for a walk behind the buildings on the property, and they chased the wild bunnies and barked at the birds. They never came close to catching the wild bunnies, but they tried every time they saw one.

My wife was home by five, and it was great to see her. I poured her a glass of wine and a stiff drink for myself and started to give her a play-by-play story of what had transpired over the past two days. I did stop to get her another glass of wine and another drink for myself partway through the narration that I had for her to hear. I told her I had a briefcase full of paperwork I needed to read, and she was welcome to read it, to which she quickly responded, "That won't be necessary."

We finally ate supper, and both of us were into our pre-bed naps in the recliners. We woke, and I took the dogs out for the last potty break of the day. Both of us were in bed quickly and asleep before we knew it.

Chapter Eighteen

Saturday morning was spent at work getting all my tools ready to load and take home. There wasn't anything to work on, so I accomplished what I needed to in about an hour. I would have the shop foreman look through my boxes on Monday before I load them. Keeping the news quiet about me leaving was hard, and none of the upper management was around today. Finally, quitting time had arrived, and I was out of the building at one minute after noon.

I spent most of the afternoon reading through the papers, also catching a catnap or two when the context of the papers got too dull. I had gone from being in debt to being worth more than eighty-five million dollars by just signing a bunch of papers. I know the worth is not all in dollars you can put in the bank, but the whole situation seems like a wild dream. There were companies set up that did all kinds of things, and some that I had never heard of before. There was a large amount of land with all the mineral rights and water rights and any other rights you could have that went along with the land. The pages mentioned a lot of machinery that belonged there and the buildings, including the cellar. Oddly, however, there was no mention of livestock on or related to the property. Maybe there was none, but the corral setup was fantastic and made to handle any type of domestic animals you wanted.

I also owned or had interest in a lot of the businesses in town and was a silent partner in a lot of others. Most were very profitable, and some were services.

I relayed all of this to my wife, and she said it sounded like this place would keep me and the next two or three generations busy. I thought that would be a great idea but doubted the newer generations would want to be tied down to a piece of property. Who knows, stranger things have happened, and at the moment we had a sort of weak start on the second generation with only one grandson.

I also did not have the need to be noticed and for everyone in the world to know who I am. I hoped the transition would be easy and quiet. I read a story one time about a woman who was worth billions of dollars but could move through her community with ease because no one really knew who she was. She gave a lot of money to different projects, and her name was known in the area, but all her work and donations were done through her company and those were the people who were seen. From what I have seen, this company will probably keep my identity as quiet as possible and continue to work with the community as they have before. I hadn't asked Leslie if Christopher was a man about town and wanted the attention or not.

Saturday evening, we started to watch the DVD I had brought home. The longer we watched the information, the more awestruck we both became. There was a lot of information about the property and the surrounding area. There was also a lot of information about all the assets and holdings of the company and its ideas to make the community stronger and self-sufficient. My wife finally asked me to turn it off as she had all the information she could handle for one day and would watch more as she got it all straight in her head. I had the same problem, and I had been through most of this before. We went to bed but found it hard to fall asleep with all of that information buzzing around our heads.

We did manage to sleep in the next morning, but only to about seven o'clock. We talked about moving, packing, quitting jobs, and wondering if my kids would be interested in moving closer since there would be no need for them to keep jobs when I was sure this company could hire them in some type of position for a lot more money. Finally, we decided to go to town for breakfast and let this stuff settle more.

We got a plan of attack written down that included getting the movers set up to pack and haul our stuff, purchasing a trailer to haul my old pickup to its new home and the start of long-awaited restoration, knowing how much time to give our employers about quitting (I am giving them about ten minutes), and other small arrangements to be made. We felt that all of this could be accomplished this following week, and we could head for our new home on Friday. One thing is for sure: we are not pressed to leave this place, and whenever we show up at our new home, it will be ready for us.

I called my younger son and asked if he and his wife would be interested in helping with the drive across the state on the following weekend. I told him very little other than we would just be taking the two vehicles—his mom in her car with the dogs and me in my pickup with a trailer in tow. I told him we could use the relief drivers, and I would make the flight arrangements to get them back home on Sunday afternoon.

He seemed a little confused, but after a conversation with his wife, he said they would help us. He had a lot of questions, and I told him we would buy them supper on Wednesday evening and fill them in on what had transpired. He said that would be fine, and we settled on a restaurant on the north side of Denver.

We would give them a little of the information as we understand it, but not too much to think that we had lost our minds. I was sure there will be a phone call to his brother to see if he knows anything or if maybe his mom and I had totally lost our minds. We may even get a call from our oldest son to see what info he can pry out. Keeping a secret from them was kind of fun as they have kept a few from us.

The rest of the day was spent coming up with more and more things to go on the list. By the end of the day, the list had grown quite a bit. Many of the things on the list would have to wait until morning when these businesses could be contacted and many fell off the list as they answered themselves.

My wife couldn't stand it any longer and gave in to calling my older son. As most of the time, the call went to his answering machine, and she left a short nondescript message that she would call later.

Chapter Nineteen

Monday morning, the most dreaded day of the week most of the time. This was the first one in a long time that I really couldn't wait to get started. We both left at our normal time, and the shop manager was the only person at my workplace, or should I say, my ex-workplace. I handed him my employee's manual and letter of resignation. His reaction was to ask "What is this?"

I explained I was terminating my employment as of this moment and as soon as he checked my toolbox and I signed any paperwork, I would be loaded and gone.

He asked, "You are not giving us two-week notice?"

I replied, "If you were going to fire me or lay me off, you wouldn't give me any time."

He agreed, and we went to look at my boxes to make sure nothing that belonged to the company was in them by mistake. By then, the owner had arrived. As I was getting my boxes ready so I could manage them when I went to unload them at home, the shop manager went up to let the boss in on the news. The rest of the employees arrived and wanted to know what was going on. I gave them a real minor explanation and continued to load my tools and personal belongings. The shop manager returned and asked me to go talk to the owner.

This meeting was cordial, but he got the least amount of information than any of them. The office manager showed up with all the paperwork to sign and to make sure they got their keys and employee's manual.

With all that handled, I said quick goodbyes and left in my truck with all my belongings. For some unknown reason, I felt the urge to distance myself from these people, some who I had worked for and worked with for over eight years. Putting an end to this chapter of my life felt really good!

On my way home, I called my wife, and all I got was the answering machine. I was sure her employers would be buzzing around trying to figure out how to cover her loss and force her to stay the full two weeks to train someone else to do her work. As with most companies, your bosses really do not know all you do for the company until they are faced with replacing you and find out what a great asset you really were and how much you did for your immediate supervisor. The crazy thing is your immediate supervisor doesn't even know.

I arrived at home and unloaded my toolboxes and returned the tools to its regular drawer. I didn't get too carried away with getting this stuff all put away, because I would be loading it back up for the trip in a couple of days. I really don't know why I am taking these when there are already more tools there than I could ever need. Maybe I am a tool hoarder at heart.

I redialed my wife's number, and this time was greeted by her cheery voice. I asked how it went, and she said they were really buzzing. She said they really need her to stay for the two weeks and train her replacement. She told them they had until Thursday night, and that was it.

She asked, "What are they going to do, fire me? Even if they hold up my pay, I think we can make it by."

We talked a couple of minutes about my termination, and then she said she had to get to work.

It would have really been great if all of this had taken place about thirty years ago, but I guess there was a lesson we had to learn.

Chapter Twenty

By midmorning, I made all the arrangements to meet with the movers this afternoon and made all the calls to anyone I needed to. I decided to go look at trailers that would haul my old Dodge truck across the mountains and place it with the other vintage vehicles that were now housed on the second floor of the old cellar. A lot of time was needed to get this truck done, but I thought I may have some spare time. I went to the nearest trailer sales and found they were very proud of their units, and I believed overpriced by a couple of thousand dollars. The next place was more down to earth, and they had a trailer that would suit my needs exactly. I paid cash for the trailer, and they made sure all the lights and brakes worked. *I guess I could have bought a new truck, but now I'll wait until I get to where I am going; maybe the local dealer is one of my customers.*

I took the trailer home and did a test run at putting the old pickup on it. Halfway through the loading process, I remembered that the wide tires on the front of the old pickup wouldn't fit between the wheel wells, so I backed it off and installed a couple of skinny spare tires I had in the shop. With that accomplished, I got back on the trailer I went and the pickup fit perfectly. All of that accomplished, I backed it off the trailer and returned the old pickup to the enclosed shop area for the day.

The movers showed up at their scheduled time and before long gave me an estimate to pack and move our belongings. It was agreeable, and they said they would be there on Thursday to pack and on Friday to load out. The load would be at our new residence on Monday evening. I told them that was fine as I wasn't sure where all of our belongings were going to end up. I had to remember this house was fully furnished as well as the other house on the property.

My wife and I would haul our valuables across in the two vehicles we were going to drive, and we could pack a few clothes to get us by.

"Hell, maybe we would buy some new ones if we had to," I said to the dogs.

Over the years we had been married, we had moved eighteen times. Each time we had more stuff. To just tell someone to "do it" and walk away without worrying about paying for it or the cost felt quite strange.

After arranging all of the busy work, I decided to go to my shop and piddle around. Pretty soon, however, it became apparent to me that most of what I thought about doing was of no consequence as it was no longer needed or could be finished at a later date at the new place. *Damn, rich man's boredom!*

I started to fill the back of the old truck with my tools and tucking in everything tight. I had purchased a dozen plastic tubs and filled them. I started a stack of items at one end of the shop, so the movers could load this stuff as easily as possible on Friday. Most of the stuff wasn't heavy, but some would take a couple of very strong backs. All the shelves were going to be disassembled and ready to load, why I still don't know, but they were going to make the move.

By the end of the day, the shop area was ready to be loaded on the moving truck, and my old truck was filled with all the great treasures I had been gathering for over forty years. Many of these items are great yard sale items and probably end up in one later this spring.

My wife came home and checked out the progress of the move assembly. She was very glad the day was over and had only agreed to three more days instead of two weeks.

A glass of wine and a mixed drink were next on the list. The weather had been a nice day, so we sat in front of the house and enjoyed the warm setting sun. We decided to go out for supper since neither of us had the ambition to do the cooking tonight. We fed the dogs and went to a small restaurant about four miles away. The outing continued the conversation of the day and the move. The meal seemed to take forever to arrive, but it finally showed up, and we enjoyed every bite. And then it was back home and a little TV before bed that came early.

The days went fast, and we made our excursion to north Denver for supper with my son and his wife. We didn't tell them a lot, just that we had inherited the place with a little money. They seemed quite confused, but the plans were made for the very early Friday morning and the remaining trip across the state. The rest of the story could wait until we were at our new residence.

On Thursday morning, I took a couple of guys I had met while living here to coffee and assured them they had not seen the last of us. We would be back once in a while to check up on them. Upon returning home, I hooked the truck to the trailer and loaded the old pickup truck. I got it all chained down and ready for the trip. The movers were almost done packing by noon and checked the stuff in the shop that would have to be loaded. The plans were made on where they would find the keys, as we would already be on the road by the time they were to arrive and start to load. With nothing else to get done, I began to get a little nervous and just started to look for something to do. I don't know if I could ever be able to live where other people do everything for you. I loaded all the important papers, guns, and a few other items into my pickup and made sure all was safe and secure. We had already packed what we were going to travel in, and all that was going into the Dodge Durango was set aside in the front room. My wife's jewelry and very special family heirlooms were packed and ready to be loaded. About five minutes of loading in the morning, and we would be ready to go. It was about time for her to arrive from her final day at the "salt mine."

Chapter Twenty-one

Moving day. We didn't sleep very well last night in anticipation of the move. We were supposed to leave about five thirty and head south to meet the kids, but we were on the road by five. The traffic on I-25 South is not bad that early in the morning, and we made good time. I took the I-70 Bypass and was headed west while my wife went into Denver to pick up the kids. The plan was to stop in Idaho Springs for breakfast, and hopefully there would not be much of a wait for everyone to catch up.

As planned, they caught up with me as I was just leaving the interstate, and we found a spot to park the caravan for breakfast. Colorado is not a huge state, but if you are traveling across it, you have quite a trip ahead of you. The pullover on the Rockies will take time.

After a filling breakfast, we let the dogs run a couple of minutes and split up between the vehicles. The adventure was in full swing. I didn't regret leaving where we were—the jobs, the people, or the area. We were headed to a giant learning adventure, and something was happening that you only dream about or read in stories.

My son and I paired up for the first leg of the day, because we had a couple of passes to cross. Neither is foreboding but a lot of uphill climbs with all the weight behind on the trailer. He was very curious, and I let him in on a little of the story. I explained if I told him everything, there would be no excitement at the end of the trip. My wife told our daughter-in-law the same story to keep the excitement. The drive became long even though we traded drivers, passengers, and dogs a couple of times. A long walk along the way helped keep rear-end rigor mortis from setting in, but I was sure glad to see the large entrance to the property and the front gate.

A quick code input and the gate-cattle-guard combination moved into the open position. After entering and allowing enough room for the car behind my pickup and trailer, I stopped and everyone got out for a first view. I was real curious on what their reactions would be. Since my wife had some knowledge of the place, hers was more wonder than anything. The two kids' reaction was of interest and "what is next" type excitement. The dogs just wanted out of the vehicles.

Chapter Twenty-two

A couple of days before arriving, I had called my new secretary and asked if she could make sure a couple of bedrooms in the house would be ready for our arrival. I did not have any idea what time we would be there but anticipated just about the time we actually arrived.

Since they had a chance to absorb the scenery on the way up the drive, their reaction upon getting out of the car at the house was "Beautiful, just beautiful." The dogs bailed out of the car and were sucking in all the new smells, and my son's comment in his joking way was "It will have to do." We took in the view of the setting sun and entered the front porch. Everyone was just looking at all the fine porch furniture. This furniture was worth more than all the furniture that was being brought by the moving company. I suggested we continue on into the house as I thought probably a potty break was in order. It had been quite a while since our last stop. That idea was well accepted, and I told them where a couple of the bathrooms were located.

When we had entered the house, a splendid odor filled the rooms. Our next visit was to the kitchen, where we found a note from the cook on what needed to be done with the feast she had prepared. My son jumped right in and accomplished the tasks in quick order. He was a trained chef by trade but had found most restaurants just wanted cooks to do assembly line food preparation at a dishwasher's wage.

We all returned to the front room and tried to absorb as much as possible. We then moved to the nearest bar area, and everyone was given a choice of what they wanted. This was hard because there were so many choices. Finally, the request list was filled, and we continued on to the patio. The trip had taken its toll on me, so my son and I sat down to enjoy the drinks while the girls continued to explore. My son sat in on the sauna and asked me if it worked. My reply was "I doubt you will find anything here that does not work." He got up and checked the controls, and then switched it on.

"We'll be trying it out in a little while," he said.

He took my glass and proceeded to the bar for another round of drinks. Soon, I could hear the chatter of the girls coming back from some point unknown in the back of the house. There were quite a few "oohs" and "aahs" as they came through the dining room and finally approached the patio. They were also ready for a refill on their beverage of choice. We continued to enjoy the last of the sunlight, and then the buzzer sounded to let us know the sauna was ready. The girls had found the bedrooms that had been prepared for us, so we moved the suitcases. The kids went to the sauna, and my wife and I sat and relaxed.

Dinner was ready, and the kids had just finished the after-sauna shower. We helped ourselves in the kitchen and went to the dining room to eat. The food was very good, but I do not think it would show up on a Weight Watchers diet list. The dessert was homemade peach pie made from local peaches that were home canned. Dinner took almost an hour, and we all had a hard time pushing ourselves away and doing the dishes. The gals found the dishwasher and loaded it with the dirty plates, as my son and I started an abbreviated tour of the rest of the house. We found the recreation room, and that was where I lost him until bedtime.

Finally, a long hot shower for me was all it took to put me to bed. The bed was the same one I had slept in before, and it took me to dreamland in a short hurry. My wife joined me, and the two dogs slept on the plush carpet that covered the floor.

Chapter Twenty-three

Morning was cool and clear; it would be a great day to spend on the great search of my new surroundings. Everyone slept in except me and the dogs. I started the coffee and then went out to catch up with those two. They weren't far and seemed to smell the same places they had visited the evening before. Either they were double-checking themselves, or there was a visitor during the night. After a while, I left them and went to see if the coffee was done yet. It was ready, and so I indulged myself with a cup. I had found some cups that must have held at least a pint of liquid, and I started with them. Back outside, the two dogs hadn't made it very far from where I had left them. I walked toward the cellar in anticipation of what the family's reaction would be to the hall of vintage cars they would encounter. *Things hadn't changed much, which is good.*

Slowly, the others started to stir and make their way to the kitchen. The coffeemaker was a twenty-cup max one, but before I knew it, I needed to make more. Those large cups can fool you into drinking more than you are used to. I looked to see what type of breakfast goodies might be around and found just about anything you may want to eat for breakfast, including some leftovers from dinner the night before. Everyone fixed what they wanted, and then our semi-guided tour of the outside was about to begin.

The first thing we came to was the observatory. As we entered, you could see the very comfortable chair you sat in to view through the lenses. My wife's reaction was "This is magnificent." Also there were other chairs and a large TV screen where others could watch as you went searching the sky.

"I would almost guess you could see an astronaut pick his nose on the space shuttle with this," I commented. That comment brought mixed reviews from the crowd of three.

As we left the observatory, we were met by the dogs. They had a lot of weed seeds on their coat, but other than that, they were in seventh heaven with this new place. I could not stand it any longer and took the whole bunch to the cellar. Their reaction was the same as mine the first time I had seen it, and other than my wife who knew the great prize that was about to be uncovered, both of the kids were ready to move on.

I moved to the control box and turned on the switch. As the pumps started and the floor began to drop, they looked at each other with quite a questioning look in their eyes. I think they were thinking there would be other old equipment and a lot of dust down here. When the door came to the stop, they could only see the large round area below with nothing in it, so we walked to the bottom of the ramp and over to the door with the green on it.

With a push of the button, the door began to open and the lights were turned on. There in all their glory sat the collection of "minor miscellaneous" cars. The three were taken aback a little and walked by the cars for a look. They acted as if they were glass and afraid to even touch them. I told the kids the driveway was actually a drag strip, and if I knew how to turn everything on, they could go for a run. My son was fair game, but my daughter-in-law was a little hesitant. I told them they could all pick one and take it for a drive to the front gate and back. Picking a car was a hard decision for them, and after a few minutes and a trip up and down the lines of cars, we each had a car picked out and slowly left the cellar. We gave the cars a little extra fuel pedal and were shocked at how easy they peeled out and left back marks on the road. Since these cars were from the "Muscle Car" era with big engines, very little pressure on the gas pedal gave immediate powerful reaction.

After a little playful fun, the cars were returned to the parking space from which they came, and it was time for the tour to continue. The cars continued to really impress me with their looks and performance more so today than the first day I had seen them. The massive size of the underground facility was overwhelming, and a lot of questions were asked. I told them what had been relayed to me, but other than that, I could not answer their questions. We continued on with each section I had been in before and by the time we were back outside, it was afternoon.

I noticed a car at the far side of the house, and so I went to check on it. The others went for a walk to the other house, and the dogs followed them. As I entered the house, I could smell something else cooking. I went to the kitchen and found a woman making something for lunch. I introduced myself and found out she was the cook.

"Supper was a great feast last night, and my son was very impressed with the cooking facilities in the kitchen." I told her. "He said the facilities were better than 95 percent of all the restaurant kitchens he had seen."

She blushed a little with the compliments, and it made me wonder how long it had been since she had cooked for anyone here. She introduced herself as Peggy.

"I have been the cook here for about five years."

I could tell I would have to keep an eye on my diet around here if she stayed around. If I didn't, I would be over two hundred pounds in a week or so. She said lunch was ready, so I went to gather the rest of the crowd. I found them in the other house checking it over quite thoroughly. I informed them it was time for lunch, and I hoped they had a big appetite because they were going to need it. We made it back to the house to find a complete dish set up in the dining room and all kinds of great food for lunch. This was fancier food than most eat for dinner, and she was calling it lunch. Wow!

We ate until we could hold no more, a relaxed meal, and took us almost an hour. I told my wife we have eaten more food in the past eighteen hours than we ate all of last week. She said she would like to talk to Peggy after lunch for a moment, and so my son and his wife headed back for more touring. We headed toward the backyard and garden area. The yard was not large and looked as if it may have been neglected for the past few years. My wife caught up with us as we headed to the greenhouse area and the flower garden area. There we found a lot of overrun flower beds and a lot of roses with neglected trimmings. I could see the ideas whirring around in my wife's head as she continued through the gardens. The greenhouse looked as if it hadn't been used for a couple of years; it appeared as if everything that would be needed to make it function was there. Again I noticed the concentration and determined look on my wife's face as she looked the greenhouse over; she was getting a big plan together on things to do with the garden and greenhouse. These ideas usually mean a lot of work for me. Maybe I'll hire some one or two to help her out, hell of an idea. She looked the yard over and didn't have any comments at the time.

We headed out behind the front row of buildings that housed a lot of machinery and Lord knows what else. These will become my main concern during the next couple of weeks as we become accustomed to our new surroundings. We found the corrals that were quite nice and functional for almost any domesticated animal. They did not appear to have any animals in them for quite a while. A little more looking around got us to an orchard of about thirty trees. These were not young trees but an orchard well taken care of. My son came to the conclusion there were all kinds of fruit trees here, and each had a hut that pulled out of the ground to protect from frost and bad weather. Someone gave some real good thought to many of the amenities on this place and had a lot of money to spend on them.

As we progressed back toward the house, my son wanted to know if we could go see the cars again. As we were on no time schedule, we went back to the cellar and this time rode the elevator down. The elevator was not fancy like one in a hotel. The doors and walls were painted with a red stripe where the doors close. I opened the tunnel door, and the light came on as it opened. We spread out and each looked at the cars that suited each one's fancy. My wife checked the Ramcharger out and agreed it was just like the one we had, except it didn't have the homemade hangers and curtains ours did for camping. Everyone continued to look, touch, sit in and start a few of them for almost an hour. Finally, everyone had their fill, and we left the garage and cellar.

After a light supper, we ventured to the entertainment area, and they found a movie they wanted to watch. Since this younger generation just lives to run all of this electronic stuff, I let my son do the honors of getting everything set just right. The movie was good and something I hadn't ever heard of and managed to burn a couple of hours up. Then everyone was ready for bed, and we retired for the night.

The morning came sooner than anyone wanted, but everyone got to sleep as long as they wanted. The dogs had my number for the six-thirty wake-up potty break. After breakfast, we sat and just talked for quite a while. Returning transportation had never come up yet, and my son finally asked what time our flight was and if we had to confirm it. I told him I had already done that, and it was about two o'clock.

We went to the airport, but created a little concern when we pulled to a hangar instead of the terminal. I told them I was shipping them as freight rather than a regular seat, because it was cheaper. For a while, I think I had them going. They both looked at me like I had lost my mind.

We entered the hangar and in front of the doors sat the King Air. The pilot and copilot were wiping it down, but stopped as we approached. I introduced them, and they explained they were flying the kids to Denver and also bringing back the Learjet. It had been in the repair shop for its annual inspection and minor scheduled repair. My son's eyes got huge as he heard the word "Learjet." The pilot asked if they were ready to travel, and the kids said their goodbyes and hugs started to load the plane. I slipped an envelope in my son's hand and told him not to open it until he got home. I then handed him a couple of one-hundred-dollar bills to pay for his cab home from the airport. The envelope contained the same amount of money Leslie had handed me in the lobby of the hotel the first night.

Chapter Twenty-four

We watched as the plane left the runway and headed toward home. We decided to do a little exploring of the upper part of the property I had only seen from the air when we arrived home. After loading the dogs for the trip, we started up the road that would take us up the foothills and lower mountains behind our house. Five minutes into the drive, a couple of deer caught our eye. They were in an opening not far from the road, and acted a little startled to see the vehicle on this part of the property.

"I'll bet they haven't seen very many humans up here in the past few years," I said.

"Did Christopher allow hunting on this property?" she asked.

"That is one question I didn't ask, and it has never come up before," I replied.

The dogs just stared at the deer. The older one had seen deer and elk a long time ago when it was young. The deer finally moved off into the brush for protection, and we decided to go farther up the well-maintained road, which was unusual for farm or ranch property. The road had nice barrow ditches for the water to run if needed and culverts whenever they were needed to keep erosion to a minimum. This road was probably in better shape than some of the county roads in the area.

The road took us past the lower reservoir and up the hillside. Sometimes, there were wide switchbacks to compensate for the steeper grade. We drove along slowly, taking in the scenery; this really is a beautiful country, not heavily vegetated or forested, but good to graze animals and give them protection from the weather. As we drove along, we could see pastures dotting the landscape, knowing that most of those were probably man-made and planted with better-than-native grasses.

We got higher and started driving in the piñon pine trees and then the juniper trees. These were sparsely placed across the land with some free standing and some clumped together. This area gave quite a lot of cover for the deer and elk all year long.

We continued to drive the well-maintained road and gained altitude quit rapidly. As we left the juniper trees, we started to come into the aspen and a few spruce spread around. There were a lot of large clumps and groves of aspen to begin with, but you could see where the spruce was slowly taking over. There was a little evidence of beetle kill in the area but very minor.

At this altitude, you could see a lot of natural open areas, and there was still quite a bit of snow stuffed in the trees away from the sun. *A hunter's paradise. Thirty years ago, I would have killed to able to hunt here, but not today. Any big game animals are welcome to stay.*

We continued up the road and came upon an old rustic cabin. We stopped and let the dogs run and explore. We explored the old cabin that appeared to have been home to any and everything wild. It's been a long time since a human spent the night here. The pack rats and squirrels were the primary inhabitants. We just walked for a few minutes and spent more time getting the dogs back in the Durango; they were having too much fun.

Finally, we were at the top of the property and got a very beautiful view of the Uncompahgre Plateau to the west and the San Juan Mountains to the south.

"A pair of binoculars would have been fun to bring along, but they are still packed in the cab of the old truck on the trailer." I commented. "I will have to get busy and unload all that tomorrow. The movers will be here."

The return trip was uneventful, and the great condition of the road helped. My wife and I talked about all the stuff that would arrive with the movers, and she really didn't think any of it needed to be moved into the house yet. Most of the furniture in the house was far better quality than ours. As time went on, we could move some in if she wanted just to make it feel a little more like ours instead of a furnished house we had rented for a week or two. We did see a porcupine saunter across the road and a few blue grouse on the way down.

Upon entering the house, you could smell that Peggy had been at it again in the kitchen. The smell almost made you slobber all over yourself like a dog. She came out of the kitchen and said her greetings. She said Leslie had called and left a message and that my youngest son had called and said he couldn't raise us on the cell phone, but wanted me to call him.

I tried Leslie first and just got a machine. I told her we were done wandering and would be at home all night.

I then tried my son, and he answered on the first ring. I asked him if he had been sitting on the phone.

"Just about. Do you know what was in that envelope?" he asked. "Have you lost your mind?"

I told him I knew what was in the envelope, and I thought I could afford it. We had never said anything about the total inheritance or about the monies delivered to me. Then I asked how he liked the plane ride, and he really got all wound up. The copilot let him fly in his seat all the way, and he got to have his hands on the controls as the pilot landed the plane. He was really stoked. I thought he was probably like a fly on his back on a piece of glass just buzzing. A little more conversation, and then the house phone rang. I gave my cell phone to my wife and answered the other one.

Leslie was on the phone; she said she had some things to go over with me and wondered if I would be willing to come into town tomorrow morning about ten o'clock. I agreed and told her I did have to be back about two or so for the movers. I also had a list of questions that had come up over the past week. I was sure she had the answers. A small supper, shower, and then we were ready for bed; too much fresh air for one day

Chapter Twenty-five

We left the new house to head toward town for my meetings. I decided it was time to start to make a to-do list. The place was in good shape, but some of the things that had to do with the farm and ranch part have been let go for a couple of years without any attention. There were a couple of places where the fences needed repair, and I had started to give some thought to the crops and the animals I was going to raise. *Might as well make this place useful.* My wife just wanted to look around town for shopping ideas, so I let her off in the downtown before going to the office.

Leslie was waiting at the door, and I thought I must be really late. Actually, I was about fifteen minutes early, and she was just enjoying the spring air. She had a folder full of papers in one hand and was ready to cover them.

Those were all the official papers for the transfer of stocks, bonds, property and all the rights to it, mineral, water, etc. I still hadn't totally been through all the paper she had given me in my briefcase, but that may happen this week.

She gave me a key to a lockbox in my office and explained this box contained items Christopher thought were for my eyes only and had no value as far as the inheritance.

"Just info he thought you could use," she commented.

She then asked if there was anything she could do for me or any questions for her to answer. I quizzed her a little about the househelp and wondered if that arrangement was permanent or not. Her response was only if I want it that way.

"We will work it out as time goes on," I replied.

I checked if there was anything that needed my immediate attention or something I was supposed to do. Her answer surprised me.

"Just enjoy it as least as much as Christopher did," she replied.

Chapter Twenty-six

Leslie left the room, and I decided to open the lockbox. Inside were papers and a DVD that had the label "For your eyes only." I asked Linda if there was a DVD player in my office, and she showed me where and made sure the player worked properly. I knew I would have a good hour before my wife had worked her way through all the downtown stores, so I started to watch the DVD.

Some of the things I learned from the DVD Christopher had given me in the lockbox were about the people who worked for me and the Christopher Smalliker Enterprise.

Ambrose had been Christopher's chauffer and bodyguard for many years, although he really didn't impress you as a bodyguard. Christopher wanted to emphasize that he did his job very well. He was a master in several of the martial arts, as well as some of the ancient ones seldom taught today. Ambrose was a sharpshooter with quite a few pistols and rifles. He loved all the cars, and they were his babies. He did like to take them down the strip on occasion just for the thrill of it. He was very loyal and loved his job as the chauffer. That explains why my letting myself out of the car on my first visit upset him a little. Christopher's last comment was "Excellent person."

Leslie Flemmings is the head of the Legal Department and very good at what she does. She had been with Christopher for many years and worked hard to become the senior lawyer in the department. She was very thorough, sometimes almost to the point of driving you crazy; however, she has never left him in an embarrassing moment caused by overlooked problems or unfinished paperwork. She knows the law very well and is not afraid to ask for help if there is a question. Example the "Judge." She is married to the pilot-copilot for many years, but they never had any children. She has been with the firm a long time and was instrumental in setting up the Christopher Smalliker Enterprise and all the different programs that they sponsor and carry on throughout the year. He believes the enterprise is as safe and secure from liability as it can be. His final comment: "Excellent person."

Travis Jonly, head of Accounting, is very well educated and a great man to have around the books. He knows all the ins and outs and always saves money on taxes. He can tell you where every cent of the company's money goes and how, with the laws as they are, he'll get the government to pay a lot of it back. He has gone head-to-head with the IRS a couple of times and came out smelling like a rose. He worked my inheritance so the minimum was lost to taxes, and Christopher was sure that with Leslie's help, the estate was already set up the same. The final comment: "Excellent person."

Henry Scowart, head of Investing and Resources, is another well-educated man and has a great feel for the stock market. He has extended the portfolios for the company as well for any of the people who invest through the company's programs. He keeps an eye on all the resources and is always looking for other opportunities to increase the bottom line. His idea was the financing of many of the small businesses in the community and that way helping to give back to the entire area. The final comment: "Excellent person."

Marvin Porters is the head of Security. They do not have any security issues that amount to much, but most of that is due to Marvin. He maintains the security of the computers and all the buildings, offices, and computer systems. He works well with the local law enforcement people and assists them in any way possible and keeps his people well informed. If anyone needs information about anybody or any security questions, he can get the answers promptly. He has a shady side that, if you need something handled—not quite by Leslie's standard—that will happen too. The final comment: "Excellent person."

Leann Monmery is the head of Future Endeavors and Charities. She works hard with Henry and also has a keen eye for local investments that will make the company money. She keeps an eye out for excellent investments for employees who are looking for a specific thing. She is in charge of the charitable organization and sees that the large amount given to local as well as state and federal organizations is going to where it will do the most good. Her area takes care of any employee who needs help for whatever, and she can get it immediately. "Excellent person."

Mary Doverry is the head of Health Management. She researches all the health plans and keeps the deductibles down. All health insurance questions should be sent to her; she also keeps the doctors in line.

The DVD went on to tell me that not only are these the best people in his opinion, but the people directly underneath them are as well qualified. None of the top managers need to work; most are workaholics and would rather work than retire.

"They will do you an excellent job" was his final comment on the subject.

My only meeting with them was very cordial and friendly, and I hoped it stays that way.

Christopher also gave a location in the library at home where there was quite a lot of information about the home place. He had compiled it as well as all the blueprints that were still available. The collection would be a large volume with a title no one would ever want to read. He warned that some of the information in the book will startle me and to read it with an open mind. There were some questionable practices that went on, and one has to keep in mind when the facility was built and by whom. He did suggest to get used to the place before trying to get the answers to all the questions I had.

"Many of your questions will be answered within a short time. Don't rush it. If you do, you may or will miss some of the most important things."

Those were the words I stopped the DVD on. I could see where that could be very true.

Chapter Twenty-seven

My wife and I returned home, and while waiting for the movers to show up, I started to explore all the nooks and crannies I could find in the house. I went to the basement, and it was as large as the upstairs. It had been turned into a gym and a large area for recreation. There were a lot of different exercise machines that could make you sore if you were in the shape I'm in—a full-weight setup and weight machines. There was a six-lane bowling alley with twenty-seven different bowling balls in the rack on the side. A large Ping-Pong table was on the side, as well as another pool table and a billiards table. Along the one wall were arcade machines galore and a couple of pinball machines.

There was a door in one corner that opened into a small room. The lighting was very poor inside there, but I just happened to brush my hand along the back wall and touch a doorknob. It was locked. There was a pantry set up, and the shelves were empty.

"They sure liked to store things," I said to myself. "You know what they say when you talk to yourself. It's either the most intelligent or the stupidest conversation you'll have all day, usually the latter."

While thumbing through the big desk upstairs earlier, I had found a ring of keys. I thought it may have the one I would seek for this door. A quick trip upstairs to get the ring, and then I returned to the dark room in the basement corner. *If I am going to find out things, I'll have to open a few doors.* The fourth key I tried unlocked the lock, and as I opened the door, the lights came on in the room ahead. The inside of this room looked like a control system for NORAD. All the screens were off, on the bank ten-foot long, with screens as close to each other as you could get them. There were control panels and keyboards below each screen. I hadn't seen any antennas while I have been wandering around, and I would think these things would have to have some big ones. Curiosity got the best of me, so I reached down and flipped a switch to on. One of the screens came on instantly and appeared to be some type of radar screen. It just had a line that swung around in a circle from the center. It did not beep, so I decided there was nothing moving in the area it was watching. *This is way over my head.* I turned the switch off. I wouldn't have known what to do if it had beeped anyway.

I continued to look around the room and located a door with ANT painted on it. I opened that door and found a very dark tunnel behind the door. Finally, I found a switch and switched it on.

"Oh my god!" I exclaimed.

There were at least twenty one-inch cables coming into the room with the screens, and all of them came from down the tunnel. I walked down the tunnel a little way and encountered very few spiderwebs. The light was good, but I thought there would be more webs, unless someone had cleaned it recently. About fifty yards down the tunnel, a couple of the cables turned to a portal that went straight up toward the surface. I climbed up the metal ladder and finally came to a hatch-style door that flipped up, opening onto the upper floor. It was a door into the observatory and was located on the floor at the north side of the room. The observatory looked just as we had left it, but these cables ran into the control boxes of the telescope.

Still amazed at the size of this unit, now I wondered what all you could watch with it. If a person knew just where to point it, maybe there is something out there we don't know exists.

I had given my wife a six-inch telescope and was amazed at what you could see with it. With this thing, you could see an ant on the moon! With her telescope, you could see Saturn and its rings; it looked just like the pictures. To see what it looks like with this telescope will be interesting. Satisfied, I went back down the tunnel, and after a couple of hundred yards came to a T in the tunnel, one headed down the hill and one went up a slow grade. Today, this would be as far as I was going. The movers should be here soon, and I need to show them where all our stuff goes for now.

The movers showed up in about thirty minutes, and we had them unload into the other house. There was already furniture there, but we would store ours there for now. We could slowly move things we want in the house as we needed. The garage stuff went in the main shop area for now, tucked out of the way.

Chapter Twenty-eight

Unloading the moving van took about half the time I thought it would. I asked my wife if she needed help looking for anything or moving anything. She said she was just going to get the rest of her clothes and mine; the rest would wait for a while.

Since I wasn't needed for the operation, I headed to the basement. I entered the tunnel as before and turned on the lights. I went down the tunnel and to the original T in the path. In my infinite wisdom, I decided the tunnel to the right would probably go downhill to the front gate, and walking downhill is always easier than up. There was another switch that turned the lights on for the next section of the trip. I turned it on and down the tunnel I went, feeling like a rabbit making my way underground. Knowing that black widow spiders like this type of place, I kept my eyes open for them. There were very few webs, and most of those were the one-string type.

About twenty yards or so down the tunnel was another exit up and a set of cables going into it as they had before. I climbed the ladder and found myself in the main entry level to the cellar. The cable continued up and so did I, finding myself at the base of a tall light pole. The cable continued up until there on the top of it, quite hidden in camouflage, was a large antenna. I looked around at the observatory, and it also had antennas around the outside of the building camouflaged, so unless you were really looking and knew what was there, you wouldn't notice it. *Someone didn't want anyone to know what was here. Why all the secrecy around here?*

It is not like we are at an air force base. Maybe there is a nuclear missile or something.

I returned to the tunnel after all my secret agent speculation, and decided to check out "my" new collection of classic cars. I opened the door, and the lights came on as before. There in their beauty was a line of cars. On the end of one row sat my old Dodge pickup truck that I brought across the state. It wasn't as shiny or as pretty, but I had put it in here with the rest of the classics. I would get with Ambrose and see who they send the other vehicles to for repair and rebuild.

I went back to the '69 Dodge Charger and sat in the seat. The interior was far from being plush as new ones today are, but there wasn't as much plastic either. A couple of minutes of classic car fix, and I was ready to continue down the tunnel. I would have loved to have owned one of these cars in 1969, but the going wage was two or three dollars per hour. Pretty tough to pay one off at that rate.

I continued down the tunnel and found two more exits that were just for antennas disguised as trees. No one could get in here undetected if someone was manning the screens in the basement. I finally came to the end of the tunnel and the last exit up. This egress was more secure than the others and would probably take a demolition crew to get open without permission. The last exit was at the front gate, and the framework for the gate and cattle guard-gate was also an antenna. All of this just seemed to be a lot of overkill for a farm/ranch operation in the country. I knew Christopher worked for the government, and maybe all of this was excess from a project he worked on.

I headed back into the tunnel and started the job of closing all doors and turning off the lights as I went on my way back to the house. The return trip turned into quite a climb, and I started to figure out I wasn't in as good shape as I thought. Upon returning to the basement, I turned the lights off in the control room and locked the door behind me.

"This stuff doesn't mean much to me, maybe later, but I don't know why," I muttered.

Chapter Twenty-nine

I went upstairs to find my wife wandering through the main level of the main house. She informed me there were ten bathrooms, six full and four half, plus a powder room. She also gave me the rundown of each room and the great value of the stuff just sitting out on the tables and coffee tables.

"There are more expensive antiques and glassware in this house than I have seen in my whole life," she said. "Very beautiful stuff, and most of it has only been moved to dust it, which happened recently. It has great value, but it's not something you would use very often, maybe once in a decade," she added.

We went outside to find the dogs lying in the yard, their coats coated with pieces of weeds and sticks.

"You'll get a good brush job before you two get to enter the house," I commented. "You will live the rest of your lives in peace and tranquility."

"I think I will get in the truck and check out the lower property," I commented to my wife.

"Take the dogs along so they could see more of the property," she replied.

We loaded up and headed to the south side of the property. There were quite nice roads separating the fields, and it was interesting to see how they had the irrigation set up for ease of operation. The spring was bringing out some of the crops themselves, but the dandelions were having a hay day blooming in the pastures and hay fields. I don't think there have been any crops planted for a couple of years, and most of the land had sat fallow during that time.

I came to the fence on the south side, and oddly enough there was a gate that could be opened to the adjacent property. The locks did not appear to have been opened for years, but that capability still seemed to exist. The road turned to the left and followed the fence line all the way to the top of the mountain. After a ways, you would need a four-wheeler or a horse to follow the road to the top. The fence was in good repair, more than likely from the neighbor than Christopher. I finally turned north and came back toward the house from behind the corrals. I then headed to the north fence line to see what I could see over there. When I arrived at the fence, there was also a gate in it, and it also looked like it hadn't been opened in years. Slowly, it dawned on me that the two places on either side of my property were built very similarly and smaller versions of the property I had just inherited.

I turned and followed the fence line up the hill for a ways and found the same problem of running out of road that the pickup would go up. The fence did have a small road that went all the way to the top of the property. I returned to the yard and had just finished cleaning the dogs up when my wife informed me there was a call earlier for me, and she had taken the message and left it by the phone in my office. The call was from Leeann Monmery. She asked if I would call her as soon as possible. She had a question concerning an investment opportunity.

I called Leeann, and she informed me the property to the north of my place was going to come on the market within a week and wanted to know if I were interested in possibly buying it. Without much thought, I said yes, and she informed me she would try to set up a walkthrough in a day or two.

She explained, "The enterprise does not get involved with farm or ranch land, and that was why I called you."

She told me they would be asking four million for the complete place and would rather sell it as a complete unit instead of breaking it up. There were over 25,600 acres and all the rights. The property was very much like mine with water, pastures, and a lot of grazing and timber. She ended the conversation by stating she thought the property would be a very good deal. I asked her if she could initiate the deal or if that was close to her responsibility. She told me anything that had to do with me or the enterprise was her responsibility. She said she would put together an offer and get the ball rolling on this property.

God, it is great to have someone do all the legwork for you and especially when they know what they are doing. Why would I want more land than I just inherited? I guess it beats a developer coming in and building a bunch of houses.

That was the question and answer session with myself; probably a good thing no one is around. My wife looked at me questioningly when I told her what was going on, but she decided to just leave it for now. I also wondered if maybe in just a couple of weeks of money, I was already getting greedy.

Chapter Thirty

I decided I would call my oldest son and see if he was available this weekend. He lives in Portland and works a lot of weekends. I called him, and surprisingly he answered. He was at work but between jobs. I asked him if he would be free for the weekend and if he was interested in seeing the new place. He said he would, but would need some help with the plane tickets as he was a little short at the moment. I told him to let me make the arrangements, and I would let him know before Thursday. We talked just a little, and I cut the conversation short to see if I could make the arrangements.

Upon hanging up, I called my secretary Linda and asked if it would be possible to have our plane pick up my son, his girlfriend and my grandson in Portland on Friday evening and deliver them here for the weekend. I told her I realized it was short notice, and if it wouldn't work, then she should let me know. She was very pleasant and said she would give it a try. She then hung up, and I was left to wonder about all kinds of things, like plane arrangements and land purchasing.

Linda called within three minutes and told me, "The plane would be on the ground in Portland at six o'clock at a private part of the airport. If your wife and you would like to make the trip, it would leave here at four o'clock, local time."

I thanked her and asked her to book it both ways.

I called my son back and told him of the arrangements. He seemed a little confused and asked about what airline, etc. I just told him the same as Linda told me, and told him the arrangements were made. If they were a little late, they could just call us on the cell and the plane would wait. With that little information, I said my goodbyes and hung up the phone.

I continued to look around the aboveground property and made a few notes in my notebook as to things to check out. A trip through the corrals with the dogs in tow turned out to be quite interesting. I found a small room hidden in the buildings that controlled an elevator. It went down into a tunnel on the same level as the cars. This was tunnel number 4. It was very large, and as Christopher said, it was set up like Noah's ark. There were many pens and recesses for animals of a lot of sizes, and all was set up with watering devices and troughs. There were small areas enclosed for birds and small animals. Most of the pens would collapse and go against the wall with very little effort. This tunnel was twice the length of the one with the cars and made me think I needed to check that out in the near future as to what was in the rest of the car tunnel. I remembered Christopher's instructions that the area underground was built as a wheel, and the spokes were connected at the ends. I pulled out my notebook and made a note, and then thumbed through the pages to find I had quite a few notes and no answers.

With that, the dogs and I returned to the elevator for the short trip back to ground level. They weren't too thrilled by the ride, but stood still until it stopped.

We continued the walk throughout all the buildings, and I was impressed with each one. Some were used for storage, some were granaries, and one was completely empty. I noticed my wife was in the greenhouse looking around some more, so we invaded the area to see what she was up to.

The greenhouse was about eighty feet long and sixty feet wide, with its own heating, watering, and cooling system. Some of the watering system appeared to be in need of repair, but for the most part, the greenhouse was ready to go. All the benches were above the ground level and set up to reclaim any water runoff that would occur. No mud!

She was wondering through the aisles looking at all the potting materials that were available. Just outside the back of the greenhouse was a machine made to mix different soils and manures, etc., together and then deliver a slow flow of the material inside to a filling area for all the different-sized pots. Any overflow went back outside to be recycled back into the process. This machine was enclosed to keep the majority of it under cover, but the cover rolled back to expose the complete machine if needed.

"We won't have to buy many veggies at the store," I commented.

"We won't have to buy much of anything at the grocery store" was her reply.

We returned to the house for lunch and found that Peggy had already prepared it for us. Peggy had showed up at six o'clock to make breakfast and now lunch.

"She must be trying to keep her job," I said.

Just after lunch, Leeann called to tell me we had a contract on the property next door for three million dollars. She said the original price of four million was just a number to keep the non-players away. The expensive price probably would have worked if the property had ever hit the market. We had an appointment to look at it on Wednesday morning if that worked for me. I told her the time would do just fine. She said she would be here to pick us up at nine o'clock. One thing I had noticed since moving here was when people said they would be somewhere at some time, they were very prompt.

I no sooner hung up with Leeann than Linda called. She just gave me the final particulars on the flight and the name of the place where we would meet my son in Portland. The pilots had used this place many times before when Christopher was well; he used to go up there for some type of business.

I called my older son and again, surprisingly, he answered. I gave him the particulars and the name of the building. He still sounded a little perplexed but said they would be there. He reminded me that his small dog would be making the trip, if that was okay. I said it would be fine.

Chapter Thirty-one

Enough socializing. I headed back to the cellar to do some more looking. I used the small elevator to lower me to the second floor rather than open the giant door in the floor. It went down slowly but was very smooth. After it stopped, I went to push the open door button but pushed the down button instead. The elevator started and continued to go down. I had no idea where it was going to end up, but I sure hoped the destination had lights. It finally stopped, and the lights began to come on. The elevator must have some way to turn the lights on as it was coming down to this level. This was a completely different floor and one that I had not seen before. The lights were on only in the immediate area, but soon I found the main switch, and the whole area lit up. There were also six tunnels down here, and they all lit up at once.

This level was quite different from the other. This level was very military with an assortment of Jeeps, Hummers, trucks, and even a couple of cannons. A little closer look also showed a couple of tanks and some trailers.

"What the hell is all of this for?" I commented. "This stuff looks too new to have been here since the sixties or seventies. I really don't know why anyone would need this stuff around anyway."

The tunnels were not as long as the ones above them but still were full with all kinds of equipment. As I walked down the tunnels with all the equipment, I started to notice the crates of boxes with the notation "Ammunition" on them. There were different numbers, which I was sure indicated the type of bullets or whatever was in each box. I could start a war by myself if I knew what this was and how it worked. Without instruction of some sort, I could blow myself to kingdom come.

Down the next tunnel were cages that actually ended up being jail cells with better inspection. There appeared to be about twenty of them, and each had all the amenities—the steel cot, the toilet, and bars. This seemed a little severe for the early fifties, but so far everything on this floor really didn't seem to belong to some type of research facility from the fifties. I guess it could depend on what type of research they were doing. Maybe this is part of what Christopher was saying about a dark side or things not being as they appear.

The third tunnel had a kitchen, a very large pantry that by the way was stocked to the hilt, and a mess hall. There were boxes of food and other goods stacked to the ceiling in a couple of areas. I looked at some of the canned food, and it had an expiration date of 2025 on it. That is longer than the food you buy on the shelf today.

The next tunnel housed offices and a communication center similar to the one in the basement of the house, but the equipment appeared to be a lot newer. This one also had about three or four times the screens and keyboards. I was afraid to touch anything down here with the fear it was booby-trapped or would blow something up.

One office had four phones on the desk, again each a different color—one black, one yellow, one green, and one red. I almost picked up the red phone, but after about one second of thought decided it probably wasn't a good idea. Maybe it would call Russia!

The fifth and sixth tunnels were individual rooms with sleeping quarters and a desk and chair. They were about ten square feet and very plain. At the end of each tunnel are the restroom facilities and showers, etc. I assumed that one was for men and one for women, but that was just a guess on my part. They were definitely dorm style with very little privacy from the other occupants.

The tunnels were finished off with a couple of recreation rooms, game rooms, and a large TV room with four large-screen TV along the walls. I had finished my tour and scurried toward the elevator, hoping it would get me out of here before someone showed up. Pretty stupid for a guy who is supposed to own all of this. I hadn't seen any other means of escape and was really wondering just how they got all this stuff in here to begin with. I didn't really know whom I could ask at the enterprise at the moment. *My secret for now.* The elevator took me all the way to the top, and I was glad to get above ground. I will have to go find something else to do for the rest of the day. I had enough of the underground for a while.

I walked around outside looking at many things I had already seen, but my mind kept racing back to the lower level. Just what is this place? Why was it built? Who else knows about the lower level? Someone in the enterprise family must know about it, or how many know? Am I going to just be a puppet figure run by the government? That was enough to scare the hell out of me.

Any of the locals who were around when this place was built would probably know, but most those who were of the age to care are probably in the rest home or the cemetery.

Chapter Thirty-two

I continued to recheck the aboveground buildings to see if they would give up any secrets that I should know or think I should know. I found a lot more horse-drawn equipment that I thought was old but, under closer examination, was almost brand new with about fifty years of dust on it. The entry level of the cellar was crammed full on each side of the floor ramp and held in with wire fencing. Some of the other buildings were also full of old-style but very new farm equipment.

One building housed ten four-wheelers of different sizes and configurations. some just for riding, some for hauling things in the back, and some for hauling four people around. There were also snow machines of different sizes and functions. Again, some were of different sizes for riding and some for hauling things like animal feed or packing equipment. One was a Sno-Cat style like the ski areas use, with a blade on the front for snow. (I hope we don't need that one.) Another building had portable clay pigeon throwers on trailers so they could be located at different spots on the property.

With all the horse equipment, I thought maybe I should get a couple of draft horses to do some of the work here if needed. Not too economic, but all of a sudden money didn't seem to be much of a player, at least not as near as it has been for the past fifty years or so. I will have to check into the horse business.

Then an idea hit me like a ton of bricks. Maybe all of this was set up in case there was an attack on the United States, and to survive we would have to go back to the technology of the thirties and forties. Maybe my thought of the second level of the wheel really was a Noah's ark, and all this now-obsolete equipment would be needed to survive. The security would be used to keep intruders away and protect the people as they worked to survive.

Too much! I headed to the house for a good stiff drink. This was driving me crazy.

I got myself a drink and retired to my office to look for books on the history of the area. The books were set up in the computer like a card catalog with descriptions of what was in them. I did look for some of the special books Christopher had told me about, those that weren't listed. I found books about the area that started with the Ute and came to present day. I found when they built the dams and what it did for the area. Nowhere did I find anything about the building or this place or the influence of the armed forces in the area. There were excellent pictures of the irrigation system brought to the valley with tunnels and canals, some that had to do with the local Indians and why they left, quite a bit about how World War II affected the local area, and some local heroes and local criminals. After 1946, there seemed to be a slowing of the area, as if after the war everyone just wanted to forget it and go on with their lives.

Just as I came across the book I was looking for, my wife came into the room to let me know supper was ready. She asked me if this place had some type of intercom, because it was so hard to keep up with me and would be a lot easier to just page me for supper. I said I didn't think so, but around here, anything is possible. She told me she wanted to show me what she had found this afternoon in the dining room as we headed to supper. Along one big wall were cabinets that housed a lot of pretty glass items. She said she was looking at them this afternoon and bumped a small clear button on the bottom of the first cabinet. The shelves moved one complete section, and a new shelf appeared at one end as another left on the other. After a couple of shelf changes, the glass that was being exposed appeared to be far more expensive than the stuff it replaced. None of it was cheap, but this new stuff was fantastic. My wife asked me if all this stuff was listed on the inheritance, and I told her not by itself. If it was listed at all, it was called miscellaneous house decorations or something along that line. It seemed like the miscellaneous items are the cars. She moved the shelves until the original items were back in their places. Maybe it is so if anyone broke in, they would only get the less expensive stuff. With that, we went to the dining table and sat down for another very tasty meal.

Chapter Thirty-three

Wednesday morning came very fast. Before I knew it, Leeann was at the front door. We were ready to go look at this great buy I had seen from across the fence. In outward appearances, the property looked as if it were a little rundown but still a viable place to raise crops and animals.

On our way to the house of the prospective property, Leeann explained that the realtor has no idea we live right next door, and for now should probably stay that way. We entered the gate from the highway, and it was like our place in terms of the long drive to the house. This drive was gravel only but still wide for most driveways. As we got to the house, I noticed my perceptions from the fence line a couple of days ago were quite accurate.

The house was identical to ours but on a smaller scale. The outer buildings were similar but not as many. The barnyard was cluttered with all kinds of old equipment, cars and trucks. This property had been used for the purpose above ground and appeared well used. We were introduced to the current owners, and the tour started. There were only four bedrooms, a smaller kitchen, smaller dining room, a nice-sized recreation room and library combination, and an office.

The owners have been living here since the late sixties and said they had bought it from the government. Part of the deal when they bought the property was that it could not be sold for at least forty years, and for agreeing to that condition, they received some very low interest rates. When they purchased the place, they had to bring the electricity from the road as there was none on the property, but all the buildings had been wired for it. *Either they have a generator they don't know about or were tied into us next door originally.*

This couple's children had left home as they graduated from high school and have no interest in the day-to-day operation of this place. The couple also wanted to sell it as it stands; they will take only their clothes and prized possessions and leave the rest. It was quite apparent that they may have had some hoarding problems, but I have seen worse. I could tell that these people lived a life of existence due to the fact that because most of what was in the house was there for a purpose and not just for looks. It looked as if they had a good life but had worked hard most of the time.

The women stayed inside, and the man took me for a walk outside and around the adjacent property. Upon glancing at the granary, I noticed an antenna, and around the corner from that was a cellar. It appeared to be identical to mine, and as we entered, I noticed it had a steel floor. I asked the man about it, and his reply was there were some weird things about this place, and some of it seemed like the government was just wasting money. *Either he is afraid of losing the sale, or he really doesn't know about what may go on underground here.*

The corrals were again just like mine and appeared to have been modified a little over the years. There was some stacked hay left from the previous year, but no animals were to be seen. We continued our tour to satisfy the owner, and as we returned to the house, the women were just coming out.

The owner told me their water was from a couple of reservoirs up on the hills behind the place, and they were filled with snow water and springs. He said he never ran out of water even over the past couple of years when there was a drought. He said none of the equipment was new, but was in "pretty good shape." Those three words usually scare me, but at this point, it really doesn't make any difference as the equipment will probably be replaced in the near future.

I pulled Leeann aside and told her to continue with the process. I thought this was a good buy even though it was a little run-down. She relayed that information, and the realtor pulled out some papers for me to sign. Just as I finished the signature business and shook the owner's hand, the realtor pulled Leeann to the side and relayed some information to her. I was too far away to hear, but I was sure I would know about it soon enough.

The realtor approached me and stated, "If you are interested, I know the place up the road that is almost identical to this one is also going to go on the market. Would you be interested in looking at it? I told the owners I would be in the area and show it if the client was willing."

My reply more than likely startled everyone there, but I said sure. My wife and Leeann both looked at me questionably, and then at each other. My wife just gave a little shrug of the shoulders and headed back to the car. Ambrose was still waiting patiently as we all got in the car and headed down the lane.

We turned south and drove right past our entrance to the next one a couple of miles down the road. We entered, and this place was almost identical to the one we had just left. As we pulled to the house, we were greeted by an old cow dog that was just looking for some attention. The owners met us at the door and after a short greeting session, the women went in, and the rancher took me for a tour.

This place was definitely a ranch and with not much farm equipment around. Most of what I could see was well used and on its dying legs. As with the other place, antennas were located on the outbuildings, and sure enough as we turned to head back to the rear of the place and the corrals, there was a cellar. I inquired about the cellar, and so we stopped by it. It was full of stuff, Lord knows what kind, but completely full. One spot in the middle of the floor was clear, and as I rubbed it with the toe of my shoe, I could tell it was a steel floor. Again I asked this owner about it, and his response was similar to the first.

We continued our tour, and there were no surprises to be had. This man's story was the same as the first, almost every word, except he and his wife had never had any children. He had raised cattle, and the other neighbor had raised sheep and hogs. On the other place was a complete slaughterhouse with coolers. They would sell their meat locally, but as time went on, most of their customers left.

"We gave them organic before there was organic," he stated. "If you buy this place, you get everything. We will load our clothes, a few prize items, and our dog and we will be gone. I talked to Joe, the owner of the other place, and if you are willing to make the same deal, this place is yours."

As he was talking, we came to a place where you could see one of the pastures. In the pasture was a herd of beef cows with their calves. A couple of calves were complaining because they had misplaced their mothers.

"I believe you have a deal," I said as we headed back to the house.

When we arrived at the house, I told Leeann what I had agreed to and to have the papers drawn up. She just smiled at me and handed me a pen and the paperwork.

"I would have been real surprised if you would have passed this up," she commented.

"Do these people know we are their new next-door neighbors?" I asked.

"They do now" was her reply.

With the papers signed and sealed, we had Ambrose take us home and leave us to my madness.

I had told my wife a month ago that I would like the universal forces to "wow" me.

As I walked into the house, I said, "I have been wowed."

I decided to look at my place from the aerial views available on the computer. I wanted to see what it was like before and after I had made my prospective purchases earlier this morning. A quick look at the address was just a little puzzling. The screen showed properties to the north and south of the ones I had just contracted for, but for those two and my current property, it stated the photos were not available. I tried a couple of different sites for this information and got the same answer each time. I guess I will have to try tomorrow.

My next call was to the accountant to see if he would tell me the best way to pay for this prospective purchase. He was very much aware of my financial status at the moment since the inheritance was only a couple of weeks old and would hopefully give me some very good news about what I had just done. I could tell that having money so available could create some problems. I was going to have to keep an eye on myself and quit these spontaneous purchases.

The accountant was already working on the solution when I called, telling me Leeann had asked him to check it out and let me know. His solution was quick and easy: selling some slow performing stocks and utilizing others to their fullest. He also told me the tax advantages to owning that much land and increasing my total acreage ownership would almost save me the amount I paid for it in other taxes in the next couple of years. He was very impressed with my decision and would start the process, so the monies would be ready for the closing in two weeks. *Damn, that's fast. Within two weeks of inheriting a bundle of assets, I double the acreage of ownership in a couple of weeks, and this is crazy.*

Chapter Thirty-four

After buzzing around for a little while, I finally settled down and went back to the project I had started a couple of days ago. I went to the office and found the book I looked for the other day. I took it from the shelf and set it on the desk. I opened it to find many blueprints folded very neat and tight like very thick pages. This was something that would answer my questions as well as anything. There was a brief excerpt of when the property was purchased and from whom. It only stated that the U.S. government was the purchaser. It did not state any particular branch of the government.

The first drawing was of the house and the description of the basement and main floor. There were a couple of strange notations and references to hydraulic drawing number 34 on the page, but that was all. It showed the tunnel I had found going to the observatory and noted points beyond there.

"This would have saved me a lot of steps the other day, but I need the exercise," I said out loud.

My wife was going by the door and asked me whom I was talking to. I just said I was talking to myself.

Further pages showed all the tunnels and its destinations. Many seemed way out of the realm of common sense, but someone had a mission when this was built. Other pages showed the cellar and the first floor below ground level. Those tunnels were configured in a wagon wheel arrangement with six spokes, and then a tunnel around the outside edge connecting the spokes together as a band on a wheel. All the tunnels were the same dimensions with the same specifics as to size and construction. Another quick notation on the type of construction was a notation of the type of cement to be used. The type only said 2-116 DT concrete for the entire complex, but no explanation here of what that means. Probably any contractor could tell just from the type.

Each spoke was numbered, and number one was north. They were then numbered right to left, which I found a little backward. Most of the words, with few exceptions, were numbered from left to right, the same way we read. I am sure there is a good reason, however. The color dots must have been added later to eliminate the confusion.

I then came across another drawing for the second floor under the cellar. It was also configured as a wagon wheel but smaller in diameter. The length on its tunnels was only about half as long as the first-floor tunnels. These also had the outside ring to connect them. There was a notation of an elevator in tunnel 5 that came into one of the second-wheels tunnels.

"Now I know how they get all that stuff in there, but no notation as to why," I said out loud again.

Number Five was the tunnel door that Ambrose had said didn't work. Either he does not know or feels he cannot trust me with the information yet. All this construction was done at the same time; therefore, they must have had a big master plan for this complex.

A continued look through the book revealed information, mostly technical, about pumps, generators, sewage treatment, the remainder of the utilities and how it worked. There were copies of service contracts with the government agencies on repair and parts availability. It was real apparent a private individual can own this place, but the government still has its hands in the pot.

Knowing when this was built made some sense to me, but why it was built in this part of the country didn't. In the late forties and early fifties, the U.S. government was real worried about nuclear war and maybe retaliation. President Eisenhower was a real stimulus to the complete country with the building of the interstate highway system and a lot of bomb shelters for the heads of the government to escape to. This one is way too far from anywhere for the people to get here and for whom it was intended. The military presence really makes me wonder. Another curiosity: both owners on either side of my place had told me they were in the army, and when they got out, they bought their land. Both had the same restrictions on the purchase and how long they had to own it. Both got exceptional interest rates, and maybe grants, to keep this land tied up for at least forty years.

This complex—and now that terminology is more correct than I know or suspect—was originally made to be self-sufficient with all of its utilities, storage, Noah's ark, and all the equipment that could be run by real horsepower. It was made to accommodate probably forty to sixty occupants in relative comfort with some being treated quite nicely.

These blueprints don't indicate if the two properties I just contracted for are included or built the same, but I have a stinking suspicion that when I go looking over those places, there will be some of the same going on there.

Sometimes I find if I get really caught up in this stuff, I could get real paranoid and start to really let my mind go wild. Before I know it, there may be UFOs in one of the barns. I decided it was time to go find something else to do for the rest of the day, and maybe check out the entertainment area for a good movie to watch tonight.

Chapter Thirty-five

Both of us decided to make the flight to Portland to pick up the passengers we had scheduled. Ambrose picked us up in the Caddy and delivered us to the airport. When I made all these arrangements, I didn't ask which plane we would be taking. The King Air was large enough to handle all of us, and I had never even seen the Learjet. We were unloaded at the small hangar door. When we entered the hangar, the Bell and the King Air were both inside. A jolt of excitement hit me as I looked out the hangar door and saw the Learjet sitting ready to go to work. I glanced at my wife, and her eyes were wide as she looked the beautiful plane over.

The jet glistened in the sun, and it had a red nose with tapering red stripes down the sides. It shone like a gem in the sun. We slowly walked toward it and were finally met by John Flemmings. He would be the copilot today and told us if we were ready, we could board and the trip would begin. We entered the plane, and the interior was plush beige color and appeared to be leather. There was the configuration of seats facing each other with a couple of benches behind it. A quick touch of the leather, and we picked two seats side by side across the aisle from each other. The door closed, and another adventure of the rich and not-so-famous was about to begin.

The engines started, and we taxied to the runway. Again, there was no waiting; we took off to the south due to the wind. A voice came over the intercom and said we would be flying over the house in a minute or two, and since my wife had not seen it from the air, they thought she would enjoy the view. Within a couple of minutes, we were above the house, and they turned easily so she could get a great view. She just sat and absorbed it all. Then another slow turn, and we were off to Portland. Those kids are going to be shocked. I hoped my younger son had not let all the beans out of the bag, but he hadn't seen the Learjet, just heard about it.

The trip was smooth and very relaxing compared to commercial flights. Now I knew why the big companies all have their own private jet.

After a pleasant landing, we taxied to a quieter part of the airport. On this tarmac were quite a few expensive planes tied down, and a few had people working around them as if they had just landed or were getting ready to leave. We parked by one hangar with no name of any business or anyone around. A fuel truck immediately showed up. After we left the plane to walk around, the Learjet was fueled.

My wife called my son to see how their trip to the airport was going, and he said they were just a couple of minutes away. Knowing him, that meant at least ten minutes. My assessment was wrong this time, and I was glad. They arrived and after the hello hugs, we helped them with their luggage and their small dog that was in a kennel. I told my son the plane was an old one but seemed to fly well. As we came around the building from the parking lot, he just about died.

"You call that old?" he said with a higher-than-normal pitch of his voice.

"I was just kidding you. I thought your younger brother would have maybe spilled the information of this airplane, but he hasn't seen it."

The fuel truck had finished, and we headed to the plane. I introduced everyone, and the copilot took the luggage to put in the cargo compartment. The copilot saw the size of the dog and chuckled as my son boarded the plane.

"Is there anywhere special for this kennel?" my son asked.

"Back on the back wall of the cabin is a small 'D' hook you can attach it to. Does your dog fly much?"

"No, this is her first time," my son replied.

"I think she will do fine. It is a good day for flying and very smooth on the way up," John replied.

The rest of us picked a seat. My son continued to buzz about the plane and wanted to know everything there was to know. As with the other kids, we kept some of the good stuff from them, so they would be impressed with what we had. Needless to say, with him talking and my wife talking to my grandson, my son's girlfriend and I had little to add to the conversation.

A couple of hours later, we were landing at the airport, and as we pulled up to the hangar, a limo pulled onto the tarmac. Ambrose got out and helped us with the dog and luggage. My son motioned to the car with "What the hell is this?" questioning look and all I could say was "I didn't know we had one of these." The look on everyone's face was registered by Ambrose, and I saw a big smile as he turned to close the door to leave.

The trip through town was quick, and before you know it, we were at the ranch. Since it was dark, there wasn't the chance to stop and look as there was before. These kids would have to wait until the morning. We were greeted by the dogs at the door, and Peggy had cooked up something for supper that the aroma made your mouth almost drool. I quickly explained where the restrooms could be found, and I checked to see when supper would be ready. Peggy informed me we had about a half hour, just enough time for a cocktail before supper.

We introduced the resident dogs to the newcomer, and after the traditional growl and sniff, they all were sent outside. I took my son to the bar and let him pick out what he wanted. He picked a strange-looking bottle and said he always wanted to try that liquor, but was way too expensive. The girls settled for a glass of wine, and my grandson got a Shirley Temple or a Roy Rodgers.

Over supper, my son continued to quiz me about all he had seen and was seeing. I informed him he had only seen the tip of the iceberg, and once we go outside, he would have another thousand or two questions to ask. I informed him I had a contract on each of the properties to each side of this one and the approximate size of those.

I told him the eventual size of all the properties, and he commented quite loudly, "Over one hundred thousand acres. Are you trying to become the largest landowner in the state?"

I thought his eyes were going to pop out for a minute, and tried to change the subject to something mellower. His mother told him about the greenhouse and how she would be looking for suggestions on what to grow. We had a small greenhouse before, so his question was about the size of the new one. When she told him, he gave us a look that said something to the effect of "You are kidding me."

I asked him if his brother had called him after his trip here, and he replied he had, but he didn't tell me much. He had told me it was a small place in the country with a little land to farm and has animals. My younger son has a good shot of orneriness in him.

After supper, I turned the kids loose with my wife to get a tour of the house while I thought of something fun to do in the morning. The tour took a good hour, and as they returned to the living room, they had a few more questions. The primary one was if the sauna worked, and they were glad to hear it did. My five-year-old grandson had gotten bored with all the talk, and so his grandma took over her chore to keep him going until bedtime. We turned the other two loose on the sauna.

A couple of hours later, we ended in the recreation room and as Grandma was putting my grandson to bed, I told them if they wanted, tomorrow morning we would go up to the cabin next to the reservoir and do a little fishing. I had no idea if there were any fish there, but to try fishing would be fun. The weather had been nice, and I thought it would be a break from the overload of things on this property. Fishing sounded agreeable to them, and we all headed to bed. Introducing the kids to our new world had made for a fun but long afternoon.

Chapter Thirty-six

The weather had been really nice and warm all week, and the fishing trip fit right in with the daily plan. I hadn't been to the cabin next to the reservoir, but I hoped it was in better shape than the one we had visited earlier. My grandson and I went to the garden area and dug up some worms for the trip. These worms were very healthy looking and may be able to wrestle a fish by themselves.

Twelve years had passed since we had gone fishing, so our gear was not in very good shape. We gathered a few things from the main house pantry and loaded all the dogs, kids, and adults and started the trek up the mountain. The wildlife was out today, and we saw a lot of deer, grouse, and even a few wild turkeys along the road and in the pastures and trees.

When we reached the road that went to the cabin and the reservoir, we turned in and drove the short distance to the cabin. From the outside, it appeared to be rustic and had been there for a long time. We got out of the truck, and I took my key ring to go unlock the cabin. Luckily, almost everything on the property was keyed the same, so the first key worked. As I opened the door, I was astonished at what the interior looked like.

"Wow, this was not what I thought it would look like," I said.

Everyone came to the entrance door and looked inside. It was not your run-of-the-mill cabin. The cabin was far larger than it looked and had a huge front room. Along one wall was a stone fireplace with about a six-foot mantle. The fireplace hole itself was about four feet wide and three feet deep. If it was burning, I think it would heat most of the cabin with no problem.

It was finished in varnished pine logs that had hardwood floors with large area rugs all over it for more comfort. The spacious kitchen was open, and all the appliances appeared to be very close to being brand new. The refrigerator looked like it would hold a month's worth of groceries.

The furniture was covered, but when I pulled the covers off, it revealed very high quality furniture that appeared to be almost new itself. There wasn't a speck of dust, and it seemed the housekeeper may have left about half an hour before we arrived.

There were four bedrooms with each having its own bathroom and a general bathroom off of the living-dining room combination. The bedrooms had large beds and dressers.

"It would be real hard not to make this the permanent residence," I said to the kids.

On the walls were many photos taken by Christopher, and many were of wildlife taken on the property. He appeared to be quite a photographer and had a unique outlook on the scenery. Something about them all seemed the same, but I couldn't figure out what it was. I made that comment, and everyone seemed to agree with me.

"It was like he was looking for something special in all the backgrounds," I said.

The upper floor was a loft where you could have a cup of coffee to watch the day come in one end or watch it leave out of the other. It was a pleasant area for hot butter rum on a cold snowy day or just a warm blanket and a book on a rainy day.

After looking the house over, I looked in the large closet on the front porch. Inside, I found a very large and expensive selection of fishing gear from fly rods to reel type and bins of spinners and lures. I wouldn't know what to do with the fly rod, but maybe my sister from Canada could come down and show me. She ties flies for a living and would probably gladly come down and catch a few of these fish. *I hope there are fish in this pond.*

My son and I took a walk around the reservoir to make sure there was no immediate danger to my grandson and to give the dogs some exercise. His dog stayed at the cabin to keep those people company. There was a nice beach area on the shore by the cabin. As we walked around the edge, there were more stumps and rocks, and on the end, they had dammed up more rock and dirt. A makeshift road went across the top and down the hill to some unknown place. That would have to be a future excursion.

Upon reaching the cabin, we all got set up with rods and headed out to fish. We made my wife fix lunch, so maybe we would have a chance at the biggest fish. She always catches the biggest fish with the crappiest equipment. Finally, she yelled at us, and we attacked lunch. Fishing went well after lunch, and after a few hours we decided we had enough for the masses.

I called Peggy and told her we were going to spend the night at the cabin, so she wouldn't cook another meal. She offered to come up and cook the fish like she did for Christopher, but I told her my wife would do that, and she should go take in a movie and take the night off.

The rest of the afternoon was spent with everyone just doing their own thing, such as hiking, skipping stones, taking in the immediate scenery or even, for me, slipping in a short nap. While walking around the cabin, I noticed an antenna like the ones at the main house hiding in the trees. The antenna was well hidden, and I just saw it by accident. No one else noticed, and I did not point it out. Hidden antennas are part of this place that doesn't need to become common knowledge until I figure out just what is going on.

Everyone but me decided to cook supper, and I was perfectly fine with that. I decided to do a little exploring in the basement to see what surprises it held. There was another fireplace like the one upstairs and overstuffed chairs and couches, a large flat screen TV, a game table that would convert into a card table, and a nickel slot machine. *Maybe a good way to make a little revenue.*

Toward the back of the basement was a storage closet, and if you looked real close, there was a sliding door in the back of it. Behind the sliding door, much to my surprise (Ha!), was a three-foot panel with a couple of blank screens and a box with many switches on it. I looked at the switches to see if there was any indication as to what they were for. The notations were of different buildings on the main house and yard area.

"I wonder why all this appears to be in excellent shape. There are no cobwebs or dust anywhere," I mused.

It appears like someone keeps this space spotless.

"I may be the warden, but the prisoners have all the secrets," I said.

Back upstairs, the cooks were hard at it in the kitchen, and my grandson was getting quite bored. Keeping a five-year-old busy without toys is hard, so both of us went on a witch hunt to find something for him to do. We finally located some paper and pencils to keep him busy, not the best, but it would have to do for now.

A very nice supper, a fire in the fireplace, and a large enough collection of books in the bookcase kept everyone occupied for a while. We talked about how my son's work was progressing and how some of the art he had done was selling. He said it was a good thing he didn't have to depend on the sales to make a living, however. He was a tattoo artist by trade, and a very good one at that. Some of the pictures he has taken of completed tattoos look alive and well.

His girlfriend works for a company that has something to do with making or marketing them; I don't quite understand. The feeling I got from the both of them was they were getting tired of the hustle and bustle of their work and would like to look at other options. His girlfriend was a budding author and said she would like to spend more time writing. She said a place in the country like this would make it very easy to slip into the wonderland of writing and just go forever. My son agreed, as far as being able to just do his paintings and perfect some of the techniques he used.

We talked a little about the enterprise, but mostly what was simple and easy to understand. I left a lot of the real-involved part out for now. I told them in the morning we would go down to the main house and look at some of the wonders that were there. An early evening and a good night's sleep were next on the agenda, and all were in bed by eight thirty.

The following morning, we had a quick breakfast of what was available in the pantry and some of the leftover from supper. After breakfast, we took a slow drive and followed a few roads that were not as well maintained, but all ended up on one of the roads that go up country from the house. We did find one that went to the north and just stopped by an open park. After a quick look around, we headed back the way we had come, and on the way out I noticed another antenna hidden in the trees. After another hour of looking, we headed home because it was time for a grand tour and a ride in the old cars.

I showed them the cars, and each of them picked out one for a ride. They went out and lined up on the drive but just raced themselves and not the clock. After a couple of trips up and down the drive, those toys were put away, and they were looking for other things to get in trouble with.

Ambrose was a good judge of character and had arrived sometime in the morning. He asked me if I had found the shed with all the other toys in it, and I said I had but had forgotten about them. We went to the shed and opened it up, almost like a treasure chest. The five-year-old wanted to ride one of the four-wheelers, but all were big, or they were the other day. In the back of the shed was a small one that looked like it had just come off of the showroom floor. I had not seen it before, and I had the suspicion that it had just arrived in the past few hours. There also appeared to be some new safety gear that showed up and just in the right size for my grandson.

With his father in tow, they got a driving lesson and a safety lesson. Before you know it, my grandson is doing a swell job of running the machine, and so the rest of them picked out a machine to try. Even my wife got on one and slowly headed down the drive. I pulled Ambrose to the side after they had left and thanked him for the small four-wheeler, because I knew it wasn't in the shed when I had looked before.

I joined the parade, and we drove around and around and up and down. After about an hour, they all grew tired of that game, so we stopped and returned the machines to the shed as well as all the gear.

We looked at the observatory. If the weather stayed clear, we would come out and look at the stars. After everyone got a quick sit in the seat and got a feel of what it would be like, we continued on with the yard tour. The rest of the tour was quite boring compared to what we had already seen and lasted until supper time. As usual, there was another feast, and we were all stuffed by the time supper was complete. We waited until dark, and then Ambrose helped show us how to set up the telescope so each of us could view the heavens. He explained how to put the right info into the computer so it would point the telescope for the best view. What a fabulous piece of equipment. The moon looked as if it was sitting on the roof of the building, and the planets we could see were quite clear. Saturn looked just like all the pictures you have ever seen of it with its rings.

After the long day, everyone was ready for bed early. Tomorrow would be an early flight home for them, and they had to go to work in the afternoon.

Morning came before most were ready. We had a good breakfast and then headed to the airport. The pilots were waiting as well as the Learjet, and we were off. As when we left before, we flew south over town and out over the home place, except this time we flew farther south and then came back for a second pass so everyone could see. After the pass, we were headed to Portland.

About an hour in the flight, John, the copilot, came from the cockpit and asked if anyone would like to fly copilot for a while. My son said he would, and they exchanged places. After twenty minutes or so, John sent my grandson forward to join his father. My grandson's eyes were as big as platters when he asked him if he would like to fly. After ten minutes or so, he asked my son's girlfriend, and of course everyone would like to fly a Learjet, so she took a short turn at the wheel. After her turn, John returned up front because it would not be long before we go into Portland.

We landed as smooth as ice and returned to the same hangar as before. We all departed, and as before they topped off the tanks as we walked everyone to the car. After goodbye hugs and kisses, they got into the car. Just before they left, I gave him an envelope and told him not to open it until he was at home. This package was like his brother's and the one I received from Leslie the first night. I thought it may take the edge off of making payments and get them ahead of the game. Maybe they would move to the new homestead and raise a family, as was my wish for my other son as well, because within a couple of weeks we will have five houses, and they could take their pick.

Partway home, we got the same treatment with the flying, and my wife went first. She wasn't too crazy about flying, but this trip had seemed to have cured part of that. We both had fun and really got to talk to John for the first time alone. He was very pleasant and loved what he did. It was a shame his wife hated to fly as this would have been an excellent opportunity to travel for them.

When we arrived, there was a phone message waiting on my cell phone. My oldest son asked if I had totally lost my mind and to call them when we got home. I gave him a quick call, and it went directly to the answering machine.

"He'll call later," I said to my wife.

She agreed. About five minutes later, he called and wondered if I had totally lost my mind. I told him to spend the money wisely and that it would help get him out of debt. He thanked me again and hung up.

Chapter Thirty-seven

That afternoon, we sat and talked about this great opportunity we had been given and some ideas we would like to incorporate to extend the range of its benefits. We have more money than we and the kids could ever spend wisely, and there are people in our immediate families that really could use a helping hand. We also know of other families and friends that need help in these hard times. Most of them could use a windfall to get them back on their feet and get a handle on life.

I decided to check with Leeann on the status of our land purchase, and ask her about how to let them know of people that need help or how to get the benefit started. I had no idea what type of criteria they used to select candidates for help, but was sure anyone I recommended would be accepted. I left a message for Leann, and we continued to brainstorm for a couple of hours. We had come up with some real good ideas for the rest of our future.

I received a call later in the day, and Leeann said she would like to meet with us after the deal was complete on the land to cover all the criteria and who would be available. We agreed and put the discussion to rest for the day.

I called Linda and asked if she would check to see if I could meet with Leslie later in the week to cover and recover some of this paperwork I had been putting off. She said she would let me know as soon as possible.

The rest of the day was spent in the home office working on the never-ending stack of paper I had been given to read and try to understand. I had a new list of questions I needed Leslie to set me straight on, questions about things I couldn't find the answers to by going through these papers. Many things were here and maybe listed under "miscellaneous" seemed pretty expensive to be classed in such a general manner.

I also needed to know where the line falls to separate the enterprise and the Christopher Smalliker estate assets. I am not a whiz at all this stuff, but I am sure she can explain the differences, or the accountant could.

The longer I looked at the papers, the more I realized just how much I had missed that day with Judge Gillipi. He had been going quite fast; I was in way over my head that day anyway. All of a sudden, I had a thought hit me like a ton of bricks—the comment the judge had made that day in reference to the cellar.

He has been the only one in the immediate group of people around me that has said anything. I wonder what he knows about this place anyway! He is old enough to have been around here when it all was built and involved with the community all of this time must have given him at least some exposure!

That was one hell of an idea, and it totally took control of my thoughts for the next hour or so. So much for the paperwork.

Finally, I got back to the paperwork and found some things made more sense now, but some made a lot less. Some sounded familiar, and some must have been stuck in after the first reading.

After finishing the stack of paper, I filed it in a safe I had found with Christopher's help and guidance; this one was a large safe, but it did not contain any bags of money, no gold bars, or other surprises. It was a large filing cabinet style made for securing files for safekeeping.

Linda called and confirmed the meeting with Leslie in a couple of days.

Chapter Thirty-eight

Spring was coming rapidly now, and I thought it was time to start setting this entire farm-ranch operation to work and maybe make a little money. Not that I was in a pinch, but to do a little farming myself would be great. I was raised on a farm, and although it sucked when I was doing it, I have missed it ever since.

I looked over the entire layout and talked to both of the men that I was buying out. They gladly gave me their ideas and some future plans they had but never carried out. They informed me the slaughterhouse/packing house was still intact and would only take a good steam cleaning to make it usable. They had been having thoughts of going organic with their livestock and selling locally. The biggest drawback was that this estate had split their properties, and no one would give them access across. That was probably as well they didn't, as they didn't have the money to do the whole operation right. Both men were very knowledgeable about their places and what the local market could support.

I asked them if they knew some local people who could be trusted to take responsibility and operate these places as best they could. Each gave me a few names and said the worst part was no one wanted to work that hard anymore. I explained some of my ideas with them, and both said if they were thirty years younger, they would hire right on. I wrote down the names they gave me and left thinking these people have no idea what is under them, or maybe there is nothing here. They had been told the switches in the cellar area that were locked out were that way to keep from shorting out the electricity from the local REA.

I took the list of names to the head of security, Marvin Porters. I asked him to check them out and give me an answer when he could. He agreed and told me he would have a report ready in a day or so.

The following day, he called and said he had the report ready and would give it to Leslie; she would have it for our meeting tomorrow. I'd forgotten the meeting that I'd had set up, and was sure glad Marvin had called.

The following morning, I met with Leslie. She had all the answers I needed. The Wheel Ranch, all the land and resources above and below the ground, minerals, and water were all mine.

All the people who worked for Smalliker Enterprises were employees of the company, including myself. My monthly salary was $150,000, after tax, and was automatically deposited into my checking account she had set up on the first day. The business was set up where each head of the department was paid handsomely with all benefits covered by the company.

Each department kept a set of checks and balances between themselves to make sure all was in balance. The airplanes and helicopter were owned by the company and were available to all the senior staff upon request, with me having the first choice. There were never any conflicts because the travel was arranged ahead of time through Mary, and the schedule is checked twice daily.

A very well-greased machine with a lot of expensive gears.

All the health benefits were paid by the company for the upper management, and all employees had very good coverage and almost no cost to them. Doctors and dentists were excellent, and were brought to the area by the company as part of the plan to have excellent health services available to the whole community. Their facilities were "state of the art" and updated as new proven technology became available.

The employees enjoyed a good 401k plan with the company matching their donations. The plan was taken care of by Accounting and was making a good profit for all, even though the economy was very poor at this time. The company has very little turnover and high morale among all the employees.

I could see why all of this was true, especially the turnover business; if I had found this twenty or thirty years ago, I would have stayed with it forever.

After the meeting with Leslie, she handed me the packet from Marvin. I took it and went to my office to see what he had to say about my prospective new employees. I knew none of the people on the list when I had given it to him, and now knew everything there was to know except the last time they went to the bathroom. Some had questionable notations next to their names and a recommendation whether they should be hired or not. This was definitely a Big Brother report and kind of scary that this much info was available to some stranger if he wanted to look it up. It was satisfying to know the people you were hiring were reputable.

When I got home, I told my wife all about the background information available.

She said, "It doesn't really surprise me."

Chapter Thirty-nine

We closed on the two properties within the two-week period, and the people from the enterprise handled all the paperwork for the old owners at no cost to them. Accounting set up retirement plans and portfolios for both couples to keep the amount they would have to pay in taxes to a minimum. They took the time to explain what was going on and helped them with any questions they had. Both couples were very grateful for the free legal advice Leslie's department had given them. She had helped them with their wills and other legal documents that should be filed.

After the meeting for the closing, my wife and I went to each property and looked through the houses and the barns. As agreed upon, the people had left anything they did not want, and that was a lot of stuff. The houses were clean but cluttered. Most of the stuff was old but rustic rather than true antique.

I left her in each house as I walked the yards and looked in each barn and shed. There were over forty years of machinery, tires, and just about any kind of junk you wanted to see. I went to each of the cellars and found the switches and elevators were locked out so nothing would work.

With quite a discussion, we both decided a farm auction was just what we needed to have. I checked with Leslie, and she informed me one of the girls in the offices has a husband who runs a local auction. He was also the one of the locals we had financed to get his business going. She gave me his number, and I contacted him right away.

He came that afternoon, and we walked the two properties as well as the main place. His suggestion was a large farm sale out in the open with the household goods and that anything the rain might hurt should be put under a large tent. They would auction the farm equipment and junk at the same time they auctioned the household and small stuff. With that settled, he said he would make the arrangements and will let me know the date.

As he left, I said to myself, "This is a big undertaking."

With that in mind, I set off to the North Place to see how much work it would take and also to check to see if I could get into the wheel area below. The first level was fairly well organized, with a couple of older farm trucks, a couple of tractors, a hay baler, and some other farm implements. One tractor was located on top of the steel door, so I moved it just in case I found the way to unlock the control.

I messed around with the lock setup and noticed a slot for a key. By chance, I brought the key ring along with me, and one key fit the lock. The key unlocked the handle, and there was another lock mechanism. The second was a different key on the chain, but it did the job. I removed all the safety equipment and pressed the button to lower the door. No reaction. I looked around and found the switchboxes. I turned all the breakers on and went back to try the door. It reacted slowly at first, like it hadn't opened in forty years, but sped up the longer it ran. Finally, it was all the way open, and I slowly strolled down the ramp.

The area was the same size as the one at the main place, except the wheel tunnels were not protected by doors. I could see down the tunnels, and they didn't appear to be as long. All each tunnel had were old machinery from the fifties and sixties. There were three early Ford tractors from the fifties. I had spent many hours driving a tractor just like those. There were also three larger international tractors that had more horsepower than the Fords, and they appeared to be of the early sixties era. Also in the next tunnel were early 4010 and 4020 John Deere tractors. There was a lot of two-row and four-row equipment for the smaller tractors, and eight-row equipment for the larger ones. There were balers, hay rakes, combines, wagons, and anything else you would need to farm the lower fields of the farms as they now stood. It appeared to me that all the equipment from both places were stored here before they sold the farms to these army guys.

I was surprised that these tunnels were pretty clean, but everything had a layer of fine dust all over it. The cleaners next door didn't make it this far when they cleaned. Knowing full well that nothing would start, I tried one of the Ford tractors. I was right; it didn't even budge. I continued to make a brief visit to look all the equipment over. It was going to take a full day to get all this stuff out of here.

I walked back up the ramp and left it open. The area below could use some fresh air, and with the front door of the cellar closed, nothing should get in. I decided that my wife and I would try to get everything out of there so the secret of the wagon tunnels would be preserved.

As I went to the South Place, I stopped by the sheds at home and got a small tractor with a bucket loader. I had remembered that the floor in this cellar was covered with forty years of hay leaves and dirt. I opened the main door, and within an hour I had all the mess cleaned off the steel door and piled outside in a neat pile to be disbursed at a later date.

I played the same game with the lock mechanism and with the same result. I turned on all the breakers and pushed the button to start the door. The reaction was the same, and the door slowly opened. The area below the door appeared to be arranged the same, except this wheel had old farm trucks, old stock trucks, and old enclosed van-type trucks. There were a few old cars and pickups spread through the stuff. Most of the cars were four-door family-type cars, but the pickups were all painted an off-color of green. It appeared to be the color somewhere between army green and forest service green. It was not a color I had seen before.

As with the other tunnels, there was a cover of forty years of fine dust, but otherwise clean and organized. I had to try a pickup to see if it would start, but as before, the engine wouldn't even try to turn over.

It is going to take a small fortune to put batteries in all this stuff and get them running.

I talked to Ambrose the next day to see if he would be interested in assisting me in the removal of all this stuff from the wheels of both places. He said he would and would like to try and help me get them all running. That evening, the man from the auction firm called to give me a date for the event. It would be in four weeks, and he and his crew would be here ten days before to set it all up. He also stated he thought a consignment auction would bring in a larger crowd, and a lot more of the locals may pay less attention to the ranch. *That will give me some time to get all this stuff from underground and running.*

The next few days, Ambrose, my wife, and I removed everything that was located underground on the other two places. We found some unique machinery stored in those tunnels that was designed just for the maintenance and cleanliness of them. That machinery was moved to the main place and cleaned. Then we put it down in the center of the wheel on the main place to keep it out of sight. After all the hustle and bustle, I would see about getting the dust out of underground.

Ambrose used my pickup and brought out thirty-two batteries of different sizes and shapes to fit all the units that needed them. He also brought oil and oil filters, so the oil could be changed before starting them. He and I worked for a couple of days and finally had everything with an engine running and ready to be located on the North place. We set up an area to be used as a wash bay, but would let the auction people do the cleaning.

The auctioneer showed up just as we had finished, and was taken aback at all the machinery. He was curious as to where it had all come from, and I told a lie and said I had found more sheds he hadn't looked at. He decided ten days wouldn't be enough, so they scheduled to start the following week.

The following weeks were quite busy with all the set up and arranging of the goods. The idea of the tent was great, except by auction day, there were four instead of one. The farm equipment and outside stuff covered thirty acres, and it was set fairly close to each other. The auctioneer has twenty people working for him and ten part-time helpers. I had also hired a couple of farmhands, and they helped out when they were not doing things for me. At last, however, everything was set for the auction that was to start in two days at nine o'clock. People were allowed to come and look for those two days, and the auctioneer had hired off-duty sheriffs and city policemen to keep an eye on them. My wife and I strolled through the tents and were amazed at all the stuff that had been found on these properties. The second day of allowing people to look, I noticed a skinny old-looking man among the machinery. I just glanced his way and when I glanced back, he had totally disappeared. *Quick rascal.*

Auction day was a pleasant May Day, and the crowd was huge. The auctioneer had done an excellent job of advertising it and had also set it up for video and phone bidding. There were cars from every western state and some from the east. What little I watched, it appeared the people just had to bid on stuff; a lot of it went for higher than new would cost. All the serial numbers had been checked, but no titles were available. All this equipment were listed as government surplus. Good amount of money for our private charity!

Finally, around four o'clock, the last item was sold, and by then a lot of people had left with their purchased treasures. Most of the machinery was being loaded on trucks, and a lot of it was headed to Mexico. By dark, the lot where the machinery had been parked looked like a picked-over dinosaur carcass.

By the end of the second day after the auction, all the fields were cleaned up and ready for late spring ground work to begin. The new hands worked together to get everything ready for planting and had been watering the pastures and hay fields for a month. Within a week, they had all the land ready and planted for the first year. Next year, I believe, we will have a better plan as to what works best where, what fields need to be plowed, and what ones to leave.

Chapter Forty

The day after the auction, I was a little bored and decided a visit to the cellar to check out the cars was in order. They are such beauties and it's a shame we don't drive them more. *Maybe in the Fourth of July Parade, if they have one.*

The door opened as always, and I was looking over the cars on the right side of the tunnel. As I approached the end of the tunnel, I was also trying to find a remedy for a problem I had. After looking at the utility tunnel, it seemed deeper than this one, and the blueprint showed a rim around the outside.

I spotted a telephone on the wall and thought that odd, because I hadn't seen it before and hadn't seen any others anywhere. I picked up the receiver and found no tone. I replaced it and began to look the wall on the end of the tunnel over for a door or something that would allow me to get to the rim from this end of the room. No avail. I returned to the phone and tried it again (slow learner).

I was about to replace the receiver when I remembered a code Christopher had given me, but did not say what it was for. I punched the code in, slowly trying to remember it from memory: 46532277. I heard a click on the wall, and a small door opened at the end of the room. I entered and found the switch. The light revealed quite a large room with dirt and rocks piled up at the far corner. At one side of the room was a rectangle shape about ten feet long, eight feet wide, and four feet high. It was covered by a blue tarp.

I walked over and pulled one corner of the tarp back to see what was under the cover. There in front of me were the mates to the gold bars in the safe at the house. I stepped back in total amazement, and I felt my chest tighten up as if I had been scared half to death. I reached into my pocket and slowly closed my hand around the container of nitro I always carry with me since my heart attack. The muscles in my chest relaxed, and I reached out and took one bar in my hand. It was number 1099. I don't know if it was the last one, but there were plenty of them in the pile. I slowly set it back down as if it were fragile crystal and pulled the tarp back over the pile. I then went exploring and found the rock and dirt to be ore and also found the smelter and the form for the bars. Along the wall were a safety equipment and a cabinet that said "Mercury" on the front. *They must have found a gold vein while digging this place; this must be what was left over.*

I looked over everything in the room, but I did not go any further. A slow trip back through the room and another touch of the pile of gold was enough for the day. I returned to the entrance door I had come through and switched off the light. I went to the phone and punched the code in again; the door closed and locked with a click. I was starting to realize why the security was a lot higher than a regular ranch or farm.

Chapter Forty-one

With the auction being complete and the spring farm work well in hand, I decided to lock out the cellar for now to keep the curious out. I knew these newly hired hands were reputable, but there is always a curious side to everyone. I told Ambrose that he could still go see the cars, but he would have to use the elevator and lock it at both ends. I wasn't ready to reveal to the world just what was underground here yet.

My wife had the greenhouse just the way she wanted and had a lot of plants ready to be transplanted in a couple of weeks. Most of the fruit trees had blossomed, and so far we had missed a late frost to kill them. I had gone to the orchard and finally figured out how to activate the individual covers for each tree. When they were closed, they looked like a big clam shell. I am sure this was an expensive installation when it was done.

With both of us being caught up with our projects outside, I decided I would get my partner in crime and show her what I had discovered so far underground. We entered the passageway tunnels that went to various outposts on the property, including the observatory and the front gate, and followed it to the door to the main wheel. This door was located by the breaker boxes and was not noticeable when it was closed. The hub of the wheel where the ramp lowered into was pitch black inside until I located a switch on the wall with my flashlight. I had started carrying a flashlight with me anytime I went underground, as I was starting to worry about getting caught underground and the lights going out.

I opened the door to the cars, and we went to the far end to get to the secret door compartment. We went to the phone, and it opened the door just as it had a couple of days ago. We closed the door behind me just in case Ambrose would show up. With the lights on, I uncovered just a corner of the gold stack, and when I looked at my wife, her eyes were huge. She stammered something, and then the second time she said it made more sense.

"Is it real?" was her question.

"I am sure it is, but I don't know or am about half afraid to have it tested to see," I replied.

She picked one bar up and read me the number 1096 from it.

"How many are there?" she asked.

"I have no idea" was my reply. "I think everything under this cover is gold."

We continued to look around this compartment at all of the ore that was there and all the tools, etc., and then opened the door to what I assumed would be rim tunnel that linked all the wheel tunnels together. Wrong again! We were in another compartment that was about one hundred feet deep. Located in it was equipment used to dig and carry the ore. This equipment was as small as a skid steer, so I was sure the mining project was not a major project. We checked each piece out, and both came up with different ideas as to what it was all about.

We next went to the back door and opened it to the next compartment. It was the connecting tunnel and smaller than the wheel tunnels, but large enough to comfortably drive a Jeep or small pickup around. It was well lit, but I don't know which switch had turned it on. You could also feel the air moving through with the circulation system working.

A walk to the next tunnel took a couple of minutes, and I knew it was the utility room. We could hear the light hum of the generator as we got to the door. I opened the door and found the whole tunnel ahead of us. It looked a lot bigger now than when Ambrose had showed it to me before. A look around this tunnel found where everything that had to do with the utilities of the main place was located. The room was spotless and well ventilated.

We decided to go back to the rim tunnel and continue to explore. The next tunnel was the Noah tunnel. It was very interesting, and we spent about an hour looking it all over and checking out all the different-sized cages and how the feed and water systems were set up for very efficient operation. There were large space-saving granaries and huge areas for hay and straw. At three locations were bins for the animal waste to be thrown into and to be disposed automatically at some other location. This was set up to allow the animals to be here a lot longer than forty days and nights.

Again, we went back to the rim, turned off the lights inside the tunnel, closed the door, and continued to the next tunnel. This was one of the doors Ambrose told me that didn't work, and I hadn't gotten far enough with Christopher's instructions to know exactly what I would find inside this one. I first found out that unlike the last two doors, this one had a punch-style lock with a keyhole. I reached into my pocket and pulled out the key ring for the farm. The keyhole looked strange to me, but instead of really looking at it, I just put a key into the hole. I very quickly received a shock of electricity that made me remove the key while pulling away from the door.

"Damn, that hurt!" I exclaimed.

A closer look at the remaining keys showed one that resembled the slot in the door, so I gingerly tried the key. It slipped right in, and the lock worked quite easily. We turned on the lights and were greeted by huge bins attached to the wall with notations of corn, wheat, rye, and four bins for beans. At a spout coming out of these bins was a grinder or a mill to prepare these food stuffs for cooking. All these huge bins were empty but were set up to be filled from somewhere up above, probably the surface level. There was a large storage area labeled potatoes, onions, apples, and garlic. All these were empty but could hold a lot of provisions for a real long winter.

Next to these storage bins was a huge kitchen area with very large ovens and grills, deep fryers, mixing bowls and machines ready to whip up fifty pounds of potatoes in one whack. This area was larger than the kitchen at the junior college I attended a long time ago. Great tables for preparing meals, and a couple of sinks to clean up, topped off the kitchen area. Oh yea, two refrigerator units the size of large motor homes.

Continued progression into this tunnel revealed an area of rooms. This looked like the front of a motel with the steel staircases going up to each level. The examination of these rooms found a room about twelve by twenty feet with a bed, bath, and closets with no telephone or TV. It was nothing fancy but comfortable for a while. Each had a queen- size bed with bed tables and lamps.

I checked the top last door number, and it was 36. These looked as if they were made for survival living. The rest of this tunnel was recreation areas, fitness areas, entertainment areas, socializing areas, and an enclosed and soundproof library. A person could stay pretty busy in this place just eating and enjoying the facilities. At the entrance was a large area set to one side, totally enclosed, dedicated to serve as a doctor's office, dentist's office, and it appeared to have all that was needed for a ten-bed hospital. On one side, there was a room labeled Operating Room.

"Wow, they were ready for anything," I commented.

"I wonder what for," she replied.

On the return trip through this tunnel, there were other things that caught our eye that we had missed the first time, kind of like when you walk through a home for the first time. There was a quick flick of the switch as we left the room, and all was absolutely dark inside again.

The rim tunnel was still lit well, so we progressed to the very next tunnel, quite a stroll to see what the next spoke tunnel had to offer. This door used the same key as the last, but I was still cautious when I first installed it in the door. The light switch was in the same location as the rest of the tunnels and lit up a couple of huge enclosed areas on each side of a center aisle. They were partially made with thick glass and steel; each appeared to be a large aquarium. There was a label on each that stated 500,000-gallon capacity. I thought maybe it was water storage, and my wife told me they were aquariums. The longer we walked along them, I found she was right. This was a setup for Aquaponics, to raise your own fish to eat and use the water to raise vegetables in the long stacks of trays at the ends of the tanks.

"Somebody was planning a long stay in this wheel. I don't know if I will ever find out who or why, but I'm going to try," I said.

We continued through the tunnel and came upon two additional tanks; their use was no mystery, as "potable water" was stamped on them, and I thumped them but couldn't tell if they had anything in them. All these tanks with their storage and growing areas took up most of this tunnel. There were a couple of offices and an area for fish food, and that finished out this room.

Inside these office areas, we found a hidden storage area where all kinds of seeds were stored in a large room that was temperature and humidity controlled. There were all types of grass seed for animal feed, all types of corn and grain seed for both animal and human consumption, vegetables of every kind, apple tree seeds, etc. Attached to the cabinet was a plaque that stated U.S. Department of Agriculture. I knew there were places where these seed storehouses were located, but most of them had to do with agricultural colleges. We again went back the way we had come, and as before, turned off the lights and locked the door behind us.

The next and last tunnel opened with the same key, and when the lights came on, we were greeted with paper goods stacked to the ceiling. The path through this paper world was only three feet wide and could make you a little claustrophobic. There were paper towels, towels, toilet paper, feminine hygiene products, condoms, toothpaste and brushes, hair sprays, and Lord only knows what else. As we reached the hub end of this tunnel, there was an area set up for reloading shells of most any description and a vault holding all the primers and powder safe and dry. Underneath one side of the mass-stacked paper products was an enclosed shooting range. The use of the paper must absorb the sound.

"Pretty good idea," my wife exclaimed.

After looking at everything, we went to the main door, pressed the open button, and it slowly opened. After departing, I flicked the light off and closed the door.

I then closed the door on the car tunnel, and we returned to the house the way we had come. I almost felt like a thief when we got home, but got over that feeling fairly quickly. We were both tired after that excursion, and decided a nap was in order.

"After a nap, let's go fishing," I said.

No answer from my partner; she had already dozed off.

Chapter Forty-two

Before my life had been turned upside down and I was living my regular life, I befriended a man who had raised Clydesdale horses. He had a beautiful place with the white fences and those magnificent horses just roaming the pastures at will. I had repaired his hay baler a time or two, and he liked to talk about his teams and all the things he had done with them.

After the auction, I contacted him to see if he knew about any auctions for draft horses in the near future. He informed me there was one in Kansas at the end of the month, and he had planned to attend. He wanted to know "why in the hell" I was looking for draft horses, because he knew I knew nothing about them. I explained my situation slightly and told him of all the farm machinery in the cellar that needed some horses to pull it around.

Finally, the conversation turned to the point where I asked him if he would be interested in securing me two teams of big horses, and that I would gladly pay him a commission and bonus for his troubles. He agreed to that idea and said he would try to set the buy up with the price delivered. He also said it may be possible to have the seller deliver the animals and work with me a few weeks to figure out how to hook them up, etc. His statement was "I know you love horsepower, but only the kind with engines and tires." With that quip, we said our goodbyes and went our separate ways.

I went to the cellar and opened the front door. I started to look over all the pieces of machinery to try and figure out which ones I needed to try and get out. A lot of this machinery was made to have a team of horses on each side of the tongue.

"I guess that would be what you call a four-horsepower hitch," I chucked to myself.

The longer I looked through this machinery, the more I really became quite surprised at what was all there. Upon reaching close to the rear of the cellar, I noticed eight boxes that had harness painted on each one. Just then, I thought I caught a glimpse of something out of my right eye, but after looking again, there was nothing there. I continued to look around and see all there was to see.

Twenty minutes after talking to my friend about the horses, my phone rang, and he was on the phone. He told me he had found a set of two teams of Belgian geldings for sale by the same farm. They had been trained to work together as two teams, or as one team, or as a single horse. They were big, and he emphasized "BIG" at twenty hands and all were about 2,300 pounds. They were eight years old, all from the same stud, and their mothers were sisters. He told me he could get them for fourteen thousand dollars delivered to my doorstep, and with the trainer for a month to show me how to use them.

My reaction was a very quick yes, and asked how to send the funds to get this started. He said to just send it to him, and he would initiate the process.

I asked, "It must be a slow time at home for you to get right on this, so what do I owe you for your services?"

"Ah, nothing. It only took me a few minutes. You know how I am. I like to keep right on top of stuff. After haying season is over, my wife and I will make the trip over and check out how you are doing with them," he replied.

"I'll have the check in the mail in thirty minutes," I responded.

We hung up, and I headed to the house to get the funds ready to send. My wife was watering the flowers in front of the house, and so I told her what I had just done. She was excited and said she couldn't wait to see them. I continued to my office and rumbled through the desk to find the checkbook. Since buying the additional properties, we really didn't have to buy much and usually resorted to cash for the process or a credit card. Filling out the check and adding an additional two thousand dollars to the total for his commission, I put the check in an envelope, sealed it, found a stamp and put it on, and then realized I did not know his address. I didn't want this check to get lost, because I had put some half-assed address on the envelope, so I made a quick call to get the correct address, and it was ready for the U.S. Postal Service.

My wife and I took the pickup and the dogs and headed to town. Ambrose was indisposed today and was not around to chauffer us anywhere.

We had not planned to leave the main place anyway. I had done so little driving since the move, and to take the wheel would be kind of nice.

A quick stop at the post office, a little goofing around at the local mall, some window shopping, and then we were ready for home.

As we were leaving town, we fell in behind three semitrucks headed south at the speed limit. After following them for a couple of miles, it dawned on me that they were the same color as all the trucks and cars we had just auctioned off, but all new vehicles. As they kept the speed limit, we stayed behind them and didn't follow too close.

When we were within a mile or so of the North Place's driveway, all the trucks slowed and turned off to the west onto a dirt road. I had never paid attention to that road, but I did not appear to really go anywhere, and there were no buildings of any type there.

There was no logo on any of the trucks, but all were the funny color of green. All the glass on the trucks were tinted dark. Each truck was spit shined and appeared to be well taken care of.

We continued on home, and I realized I had left the cellar door open. I put the pickup away and headed that way to close it. Approaching the building, I noticed someone was inside, and so I slowly approached the door. It was one of the farmhands we had hired, and he was just looking at the horse equipment.

"Beautiful stuff, but I would hate to try to keep up with these places with it," he muttered.

"We're just going to play with it," I said. "I have two teams of horses coming to pull it."

"Really," he replied. "That sounds fantastic!"

With that, we closed the cellar door, I went to the house for lunch, and he went on his way attending to whatever chore he had to do.

Chapter Forty-three

This day went from great to weird at noon. This morning, the good news about draft horses; this afternoon, who knows? Just after lunch, I sat down for a quick catnap. All of a sudden, the dogs went off barking and carrying on. They wanted to get out to check on something. I let them out and followed them around toward the corral. When I caught up with them, they were about ten feet from a huge bull moose. They had decided to quit barking at him but were not sure just what he was. This is not the country moose you see, because there are no the marshy lands they like to eat from. This moose as a little agitated at the dogs but stood its ground. I called off the dogs and went to find my wife. She had heard the commotion and was headed our way. She saw the moose about the same time I saw her, and she just stopped.

"Where did that come from?" she asked.

"I have no idea."

We watched this animal for about fifteen minutes. He finally got tired of us and trotted off toward the North Place. I knew the state had transplanted some a few years ago, but had no idea they were around here.

"I think he is lost. Maybe he will find his way home," I said as the rest of us headed to the house.

Not more than fifteen minutes later, a black Chevrolet Suburban with all black windows pulled up to the front door. A tall man got out of the passenger side and came to the door. My dogs lit off again, so I had to calm them down before answering the door.

"May I help you?" I asked.

"Are you Mr. Christopher Smalliker?" he asked gruffly.

"No, he passed away about four years ago from cancer" was my reply.

"Are you sure?" was his response.

"Yes, I inherited this place. What is it you need?" I asked.

"We did some contract work for him five years ago, and he said he had more to do when we had time. We have been out of the States for the past five years and were just checking back with him."

"What type of work do you do?" I questioned, but I noticed this guy was getting nervous.

"Probably not the kind you would have the need of our services, thank you," he said as he turned to return to his vehicle.

He got into the front seat and closed the door, but the vehicle just sat there for a couple of minutes. Finally, they started the vehicle and slowly turned around and departed down the driveway.

I had noticed a black Suburban once in a while going past the drive, but didn't give it any thought. Maybe I'll be less apt to leave the front gate open as I come and go.

Back inside, I went to the recreation room and played my nickel slot machine. All of a sudden, I heard a phone ring, not the electrical sound of a cell phone, but a regular phone ring. I headed in the direction of the noise and found it coming from the room with the radar screens. It was the black phone, and I answered it. At that point, whoever had called just hung up.

Muttering to myself, I headed upstairs to find my wife. She was taking a nap, so I went to the office. I sat down at the desk and noticed a note on a full sheet of paper. I did not recognize the handwriting, but it said, "I like what you have done to the place.—N."

"Now who in the hell put this on my desk?" I said out loud. "This place is really weird this afternoon."

No one but my wife and I were around this afternoon; Peggy had gone to town, and the farmhands didn't come to the house. I had been by my desk on the way to lunch and had not seen any note then.

Maybe we have gained a ghost today. Maybe what I saw in the cellar was something more than a glimpse.

Returning to the recreation room, I went straight to the radar room and picked up the phone. When it started to ring, I hung it up. About that time, I noticed a humming noise coming from the passageway. I turned on the lights and started down the passageway. When I came to the first door that would allow the tunnel to be sealed for protection of intruders, and turned on the light, I was met by a machine coming up the tunnel. I backed up, but it kept coming. When it came to the door seal, it adjusted its size and maneuvered through the door. As I watched it come toward me, I noticed that it was cleaning the passageway tunnel. It appeared to be one of these automatic things that were preprogrammed to do its job.

Returning to the radar room, I waited for this machine to enter the room behind me, and was surprised when it reached the door and reversed itself to return down the tunnel it had just come up. I followed it back down as far as it was when I met it and turned the light off. The machine only had one small green light visible in the dark. Now I know why the tunnels were always so clean when snooping through them; this place is taken care of by a robotic maid. I watched it until it disappeared out of sight and then returned to the recreation room to see if I could clear my mind of all the stuff that had happened so far this afternoon. Someday, I will have to walk all these passageway tunnels and figure out where that cleaner parks when not in service.

I remembered the blueprint book and went to my office to find it. The book was located right where it was left. I retrieved the book and placed it on the desk. I opened to the main blueprint and started looking for the detail on the complete wheel assembly. The blueprint showed the wheel and hub, spokes and rim, and also showed the lower wheel with spokes and rim. Looking at this print reminded me of the old space station pictures from the fifties and sixties, with two wheels and a long shaft through the center. Slowly, I looked for the print of the passageway tunnel and followed around its trail until I found the notation for the recharge station where I would find the tunnel cleaner when not in use. I followed the wire diagram, but there was only electrical connections to the docking station for the cleaner. There appeared to be a dump station for the cleaner at the dock station. Pretty efficient, but everything here appears to be built for efficient operation.

After looking at the blueprint book and returning it to the shelf, I took the book next to it and started to thumb through. It was a photo album of the construction phase of this place, and it was quite interesting to look at the progress from start to finish. As it came to the area of the house, the pictures seemed to have lot of steel beams and steel in all sizes around. There was one picture of long tubes looking like hydraulic cylinders being lowered into the ground where the basement would eventually be.

A few pages later, there was a picture of a control panel that appeared to be located somewhere in the basement. As the photo's main purpose was the control board and not the room around, I took a long look at what little I could see in the background before going to the next page. The next pages showed the outside of the main house being erected, but appeared it was of metal and not wood logs. This was enough new information to digest. The books were returned to the shelf, and I returned to the basement for a look around. Looking took about two hours of my time, but I finally located the panel hidden behind a corner wall at the bar. A small switch opened the panel and really opened my eyes.

The panel was called the House Lowering Console. There were switches and knobs, gauges, and all kinds of indicators. A panel of eight indicators showed how far the house could be lowered; the full extent of that process would be sixty feet. The panel was quite self-explanatory, but off to the side was a logbook of when it had last been lowered. The log stated it was lowered the day after I had left from my initial visit. The notation on the responsible party was AS.

I thumbed back through the log and found that AS had been signing this log four times a year for the past eleven years. Before that, it was a JS for twenty years, and the very first on the log was a GG.

I continued to look the panel over and tried to understand everything it was in control of. Apparently, the complete building sinks into the ground, and a concrete shield slides over it.

"What do they do with the chimney?" I wondered. "What if there was a fire in the fireplace? How do they seal off the pathway tunnels? Wouldn't someone notice the house sinking into the ground?"

There were too many questions to answer and no one to answer them.

I went outside and looked around the foundation of the house—solid as a brick wall. Then I took out my pocket knife and scratched on one of the logs for the outside wall. The finish was hard, but one spot gave way to metal below the finish. These beautiful logs on my log home are made out of painted metal. I don't know of anyone that would be able to tell that without a magnet.

I stepped inside and checked the logs, and they were wood. I don't know how thick of wood, but the real thing. This new revelation really had me buzzing. *I've never seen such a place that looked as if it is one thing and for what purpose.*

Then like a large bright light came on in my head, *if that guy in the Suburban had worked for Christopher five years ago, he would have known that I was not him when he asked me if I were Christopher. There was something really fishy about that visit.* A call to Marvin Porters was in order.

The only sane thing that happened in the afternoon was about five thirty, when the call came in from my friend to inform me the horses were headed my way tomorrow. He told me it would take three days to get here. They planned to get to his house the second night, and he was going to have them unload and let the horses eat and relax there before the next day's journey to here.

I thanked him for all his trouble and hoped all went as planned. Usually, these short-notice trips end up with something or another not going quite as planned.

Chapter Forty-four

Horse Day, BIG HORSE DAY. Excited that the big boys would be showing up today, you would think I was some kind of horse lover. I have always admired these big horses, and the thought of them working some of the ground was exciting. Realizing I had no idea what they would need for feed tonight and making sure there was a secure pen for them with plenty of feed and water was the project of the day. It really didn't take much time to gather all that was needed and hoped it would be sufficient for the first day at their new home. They were coming from less than one thousand feet altitude, and possibly it would take a couple of days for them to adjust, just as it does with humans; who knows, maybe longer.

While putzing around checking out everything for the horses, it seemed to me that a couple of times during the morning, there was a glimpse of something that caught the corner of my eye. My sight is not the best, and when my double take was over, there seemed to be nothing. These small glimpses of something seemed to become more and more prevalent the longer we stay here. Maybe the place has ghosts, and they are becoming used to us. We don't scare them as much as we used to! This time, however, my small dog started barking and headed around the building. She stopped right after she got out of my sight and was sniffing at the door of the building when I arrived. Upon opening the building door, I didn't notice anything unusual. She just sniffed around for a while and acted satisfied. We went back to the work at hand of gathering for the welcome-home party.

After arranging everything that could be thought of for the horses, my next plan of attack was to spend some time in the office and make sure all the paperwork was caught up. As there are no bills to pay, and payroll for the help was handled in town, there was really not a lot going on in the home office. After going through a few things and growing bored with that, a trip to the downstairs area sounded good. I visited the radar room, and noticed the vacuum was running again. It appeared the vacuum ran at least once a week, but then I realized that every time I had one of those "glimpses," the vacuum had been running.

I entered the passageway and followed the noise. It appeared to be going down the passageway to the cellar, and so I followed. This is another quite ingenious tool that was installed to keep this place spotless. I have no idea when it was installed, but it gets used, and the spiders and bugs are kept at bay in the passageways.

Following its noise trail and coming to the door to the cellar, below ground level, I decided to look around and see if there was anything I had missed in my many trips to the area. Since I had found what each large spoke tunnel's main purpose was, time spent down here had been minimal. I was just ready to open the door for the cars when there was the sound of a door closing somewhere. The noise startled me, and I had second thoughts about following the sound. Someone could live quite comfortably in this underground maze, and if you knew where all the nooks and crannies went, you would be able to outrun or maneuver someone who was not as familiar with the space, like me!

Maybe my next trip down, I will bring the dogs, and they can let me know if there is something or someone strange down here. I will probably let my wife know what I am up to just in case. I also have the Security part of the company; they may know all about all this stuff and are just waiting for me to release all of it to the public. From the indications received from them, I don't believe that is the case.

Back outside of the passageways, there should be something to keep me busy, but it wasn't apparent just what it was. The thought of the sound in the cellar just kept haunting my thoughts all day long.

The event of the day happened about four o'clock when the call came in for the final directions to the ranch. The instructions were given slowly, and within twenty minutes there appeared a large truck pulling a very large horse trailer behind it starting up the drive.

I called to my wife, and we both watched as the truck came to the house. I waved them around back to the corral area, and there they stopped. The driver was a large man about six and a half foot tall. He had a voice that was not much louder than a whisper as he introduced himself and his passenger. The passenger was not as tall or as large, but still stood over six foot tall and probably weighed 225 pounds, his voice was what I had expected to come out of the driver's mouth.

With all the introductions over, they were shown the facilities that had been prepared for the "boys." The young man said they were better than they had seen their whole life and would serve them quite well. The horses were unloaded one at a time by the young man. He was talking to them most of the time. Each was tied to the fence until all four were standing alongside each other. The young man seemed nervous as I inspected the four beauties, or maybe I should call them "handsomest." Their names were Mike, Jim, Bill, and Rex. Lord knows they will have to have a nameplate hung around their necks, because they all looked identical to me.

Mathew, the young man, was going to stay with us for two months and teach anyone who was going to work these animals all about them. He would also take over the total care of them and make sure they were shod and fed properly. First on the agenda was a drink of water for them and a long walk up the back pastures to stretch their legs.

The truck driver unloaded all the equipment and feed that had been sent—just a lone suitcase for Mathew. He told me that if I didn't like these horses, the man who had bought them for me would gladly take them; the purchaser was quite impressed with them. The driver wanted to get headed for home. With a wave and a small cloud of dust, he headed back to the highway.

All five of the "boys" were gone for about an hour, but when we could see them again, they were walking four abreast and instep, Mathew riding one of the end ones. They looked like an army out for drill practice. About a hundred feet from the corral, Mathew dismounted and released the halter ropes. The four spread out and started to buck and kick their heels up. That was a lot of horse to see act like that.

"They are glad to be out of the trailer," Mathew said as he walked up to where we were standing.

"I can't say as I blame them," my wife said.

"They will get rid of some of the stored energy for now. I will feed them and put them away for the night. They should sleep well tonight after the long day."

We gathered Mathew's suitcase and headed to the house. The maid had made up a room for him, and we thought he would be ready for a good night's sleep too. He was curious about the acreage and was totally overwhelmed by the total amount. I had just told him the amount that was being farmed and covered with houses and pastures. He then asked about equipment for the horses, so I took him to the cellar and opened the doors. He saw all the equipment for the horses and after I explained it was all new, he just scratched his head and let out a loud "Whew." I showed him the boxes of harness, and he was very impressed by the quality and amount. He said by the style and name on the boxes, the harness had come from the county he was from, and they were still in very supple shape.

"If you were to order these today with this quality, it would cost between eight to ten thousand dollars. These almost look as if they were custom made for these horses," he stated.

He continued to look over the equipment and could not believe this stuff was at least fifty years old.

Just before supper, Mathew called home and talked to his girlfriend. They talked for only a few minutes, but the excitement in his voice sounded like a child at Christmastime. I was surprised he didn't have a cell phone, but his reply was he didn't believe in them. I explained he could use the home phone or any of the cell phones at any time he wanted to with "no time limit either."

After supper, he went to care for the horses. I could tell he had a great love for them, as he talked to them and they followed him to the corral. He fed them and brushed each for about fifteen minutes. I believe when he has to leave to go back home, it would be a very sad day for all concerned.

I received a call from the man who had done the purchasing of the horses and the arrangement of their delivery. He asked me if they were what I wanted and if I was pleased. My reply was that I was very satisfied with the whole project, and they were "keepers." He sounded a little disappointed but was very glad they fit the bill.

I asked if the finder's fee was sufficient and would cover any and all expenses for the complete purchase. His reply was "Very sufficient. At that rate, I'll buy you horses every day of the year!"

We talked about everything under the sun for about thirty minutes and then finally said goodbye. Hearing from him was good, and I would have to invite him for a visit sometime in the near future.

Chapter Forty-five

As with the world, not everything is roses all the time. The day after the big horse excitement, our oldest dog became ill. A trip to the vet proved to be a very long day. He was diagnosed with total kidney failure with no chance of recovery. Rather than make him suffer, we knew the inevitable and had him put down. They did it in the front seat of the pickup, so there was no public attraction as to what was going on. He was given a sedative and then the euthanasia shot. As he slowly went to sleep for the final time, he seemed to understand we had taken this step for his own good and to stop the suffering.

Gus was fourteen and a half years old and had been with us since he was nine weeks old. He was purchased at a Country General store for seventy-five dollars. This seemed like a very high price for a dog, but it turned out to be the best money I have ever spent. My wife fell in love with him, but he became my dog and best friend for a long time.

Gus was an Australian Shepherd Border Collie cross and definitely had the Aussie temperament. He looked like a baby panda and had a natural bobtail. He was very mellow, and his idea of playing fetch was you throw it once then have to catch him to get it back; one time was enough for him. He liked to watch everything that was going on and check out the different tools as they were left on the floor during the repairs. He would spend a morning on the front yard watching the cars drive by or the tractors working the fields. He reminded me of my father as he too would just watch as the world went by and absorb all of it as he could.

Coming from the herding group, he herded us all the time if he wanted to go one way and you another. He loved kids and always kept an eye on them when they were around. He liked all animals and tried to lick all of their faces; sometimes the sheep or horses weren't always receptive to that and would try to kick or butt him. When he was younger, he could outrun any dog he met including my son's black Lab.

As the years went by, and mostly the last year, his black-and-white muzzle became gray and white. I knew he was getting old and had slowed down quite a bit. His hearing had gone the last six months, so we had to keep a better eye on him. He will be dearly missed.

We found a place that would be designated as the pet cemetery and buried him in the late afternoon.

Sadie, our other dog, is five years younger. She is a Border Collie Australian Shepherd cross, ninety-nine percent Border. She is a lot higher strung and always wants to play ball. She too is very fast and normally wants to herd anything whether it needs it or not. She is suffering a little separation anxiety, and now is not more than a few feet from me at all times. She even checks to see if I have snuck out a window when I go to the bathroom. I noticed she is starting to gray around the muzzle also.

Chapter Forty-six

A week had passed since the horses showed up here, and Mathew was slowly working them—a team at a time for half a day. Each team pulled a two-bottom plow through the dirt on the acreage left for them to work. They made the work look like they were just out for a stroll, and it wasn't any work for them.

After breakfast one morning, Mathew showed me how to harness them and just what the purpose of each strap was. He seemed to have great patience with me and was willing to tell me all he knew about draft horses. About halfway through the lesson, he posed a question to me that took me totally by surprise.

"Who is that old man I see standing by the cellar door sometimes? Does he live here or just visit?"

I must have looked quite stupid as I had no idea what he was talking about and told him so. He explained that when he was working the horses, he had seen the man a couple of times, but the person seemed to hide when he thought Mathew may see him. Mathew said he never got very close to him, but what he could tell, he looked quite slender, about my size, and with sparse gray hair. Mathew thought maybe it was someone visiting or maybe visiting the other farm help. I told him I would check with the rest of the help to see what could be found out. We continued with the lesson, and about midmorning, it was time for a break.

Mathew was a quiet person, and without prying into his personal life, information about his life back home was hard to get from him. He did not watch TV nor did much of anything recreational in his spare time.

Telephone usage was a very minimal, even though he was told to use it all he wanted. He phoned his girlfriend about every other day, but only talked for maybe ten minutes at a time.

He dressed very plain and made me think of the Amish people from the area he had come from. He seemed to be quite religious, and that made me uneasy after I let off with a string of cuss words without noticing he was around. I guess we all could use some restraint in the way we talk.

As we enjoyed a drink of water and some high-calorie item Peggy had produced in the kitchen that morning, he got a real serious look on his face and fired off another time-stopping question.

"Would you consider hiring me to work full time for you? I can do any of the manual work needed around here, and I am a very good carpenter. I notice some of the houses on these properties are vacant, and I could live in one and fix it up. I would like to bring my fiancée to this area."

Wham! Wake up here, you are being questioned about a very serious situation here, and this young man is waiting for an answer.

"If you would like to bring her here to see the area to make sure she would like to live here first, you are welcome to do that. I could arrange for the company jet to go pick her up and fly her here all in one day. She may not like this slightly barren country compared to your home area."

"We don't fly," he said, "but I could arrange to have her brought here by a friend of the family."

"She is welcome anytime, and can stay as long as she likes," I replied. "There are plenty of accommodations here, and she could stay as long as you like."

Mathew almost jumped for joy at this response and said he would ask her the next time they talked.

I handed him my cell phone and said he could call right now.

"No, it is not our time to use the phone again for a couple of days."

"Okay" was my reply.

"As far as hiring you, I will need someone to care for these horses and additional animals as time goes on. These big horses are very beautiful, and I want to keep them healthy and happy for a long time. You let me know what you need for a wage."

Mathew seemed happier the rest of the day, and he kept himself very busy. I told him he could look at either of the empty houses on the north or south place and give me an idea of what he would want to do to them. I also showed him the woodshop area, and he stood and almost drooled at all the equipment.

"I could make a lot of furniture here," he said finally.

I snuck the prying question in and asked if his family would really miss them if they moved out here. With some hesitation, he started to allow some of his family secrets to leak out.

He told me he did not see eye to eye with his father, and the decision to sell these horses was the breaking point.

"I have raised them all from birth and done all the training from the start. They were to be mine to keep and hopefully use to make my livelihood for the future. Ownership became an issue about a month ago, and the decision to sell them was made without my input," he said.

The consensus was they were too large for the work they normally do and wouldn't pay for themselves if kept on the farm. The decision to send him with the team was only allowed after a lot of discussions. His father hoped a trip away from home would make him realize what the world was like, appreciate what he has there, and break the bond he had with the gentle giants.

"I could not believe this place when we arrived," he said. "It is very beautiful here, and as time goes on, I could farm more of it with the horses. I am sure that my fiancée will like the area, but for her living so far from home may be a problem. I really appreciate the offer for her to come and the hospitality offered to her and whoever brings her."

"If she wanted to stay and work, I am sure there are plenty of things for her to do here. I do not know what she is interested in doing, but that would give her additional reason to make the move" was my reply.

The discussion continued off and on for the rest of my training session, and the longer he talked, the more excited I could see him becoming. Later in the week when it was his "time" to call her, he proposed the whole idea to his fiancée and told her to think about the opportunity. He would call again in a couple of days.

As for the visitor, I checked with the hands, and one said his grandfather had visited for a couple of days and loosely fit the description. He didn't know he had come over to this part of the farm. He would keep him on his side of the property. I told him that was not necessary and didn't want too many strangers wandering around here.

Chapter Forty-seven

We spent the evening being bombarded with a rainstorm loaded with lightning. There were a lot more lightning and thunder than rain. As I watched from the protection of the house, my attention was drawn to the area that seemed to be getting the brunt of the strikes. The solid rock formation on the edge of the highest visible ridge seemed to take most of the hits, some that seemed to last for a couple of seconds. This was the rock Christopher made several paintings of, which were located in the cabin up by the pond.

The last couple of weeks and the thought of a wildfire starting were eating on the back of my mind, as the weather had been fairly dry. Deciding to get up early in the morning and make a quick run up the mountain on a four-wheeler to check for smoke, I retired for the night amid a couple of loud blasts of thunder and bright flashes of lightning.

I awoke at daylight and slipped out of the house without the dog or my wife being awakened. A trip to the toy shed netted me a medium-sized four wheeler with a full tank of fuel, and away I went up the hill. The rain had helped settle the dust, but wasn't enough to make the trip muddy and slippery. A turn at the right spot in the road headed me toward the area of the rock structure jutting out of the dirt. Keeping an eye out for any sign of smoke, I was also enjoying the fresh morning air on this early morning ride as I progressed to the rock.

I arrived at the immediate area of the rock and left the four-wheeler near a cluster of oak brush. Upon walking around, I found a couple of spots where lightning had struck, but no fire to report. The early morning silence was broken by the sound of a small aircraft in the distance; it appeared to be headed in my general direction. I stood and watched a minute to see where this aircraft went and what it was. Finally, with a pair of binoculars I had scrounged from the toolbox of the four-wheeler, I spotted a small two-seater helicopter headed directly toward me. This helicopter had been around before, because we had witnessed it flying around usually in the early morning and again in the late evening of the same day. It would not be seen again for a couple of weeks after that.

I only own one camouflaged sweatshirt, and by chance alone it was what I was wearing. Deciding to make my presence unknown and watch to see if this helicopter was going to land near here, I found an outcropping of trees close to the rock wall.

"Maybe that guy has a marijuana plot growing on my land. Boy, I could have fun letting the cops in here to cut it down and haul it off," I muttered to myself.

Just as I had settled in to watch where the chopper went, there was a rumbling noise from the ground, and a small covering over a cement pad opened up on the ground. *What the hell is going on here? What is going to happen? Who are these people, and what are they doing here? I hope they don't see me! I hope they don't have guns and are willing to use them on me!* All this was racing through my mind, and I am not sure, but maybe out of my mouth too.

The chopper landed about one hundred feet from me. The pilot let the rotors almost come to a stop. Then a doorway opened not ten feet from me on the rock wall, and an old humped-up man exited the door. He turned around and lifted a piece of the rock wall just big enough to hide a switch, punched a button to close the door, and slowly headed to the chopper. He glanced back in my general direction but did not hesitate as he made his way to the helicopter. The pilot was waiting next to the machine and assisted him as he climbed in the door. A quick glance around, and the pilot went to the other side and climbed into the pilot's seat. The engine sped up, and the small craft quickly lifted from the ground and headed to the east into the bright sunlight. I sat down next to the rock totally perplexed by what I had just seen. The pilot was Ambrose.

Chapter Forty-eight

I continued to sit against the rock for a couple of minutes until I was jarred into consciousness by the noise of the concrete slab being closed again. The interruption of the silence by the noise made me jump and severely bumped my left elbow against the rock. With a few choice cuss words and continuous rubbing of the elbow, I stood up and went to look at the rock cover over the switch. If I hadn't seen the precise place the switch was located, finding it would be almost impossible. I opened the cover to find a very simple set of on-off switches.

Becoming more curious by the moment, I pushed the on button, and the door opened quite easily. I entered the well-lit tunnel and pushed the off button inside. The door closed, and down the tunnel I went. It was more like a long hallway, but it delivered me to an area the size of a small house, about one thousand square feet or so. Along one of the walls was a set of radar screens and other communication equipment very similar to the equipment behind the panel in the big house. In what I would call the living room was a nice couch, recliner, TV, radio, and shelves with books and maps. Much of this stuff looked as if it had come from the library located at the main house, but none appeared to be a recent acquisition; in fact, much was covered with a layer of dust.

After getting blasted last night with lightning, I am surprised there is not a pile of rocks lying around. Continuing on my snooping mission, the next room was a small but efficient kitchen and small dining room area, then two bathrooms, slightly dated, and two bedrooms, only one looked to be in use.

"I wonder just why this guy is stowed away up here, and maybe he has some answers as to why this whole thing was built." I uttered.

I found an exit that appeared to head downhill, and it made me wonder if it went to the main house or to the cellar or just where it would end up. I continued to snoop and saw a switch that said curtain. There was just a plain wall there, but I pushed the button anyway. A metal curtain opened, and there was a large picture window in front of me. The view was breathtaking, as you could see for miles in three directions. I knew you could see into Utah, and maybe with some help of a telescope, all the way to Moab. I gazed for quite a while before closing the metal curtain and returned to the exit. This tunnel was large enough to handle a two-seater side-by-side four-wheeler and only went about twenty feet before it came to what appeared to be an elevator. I pushed the button, and the door opened up. Stepping inside, I saw a board with four buttons. I decided to play "What's behind door #3" and pushed number 3. The elevator came to life, and I started the trek down. It was a heavy-duty elevator made to carry heavy loads up and down, and it lumbered along at a slow pace.

The cage made the stop at number 3, and the door opened. Unlike most anything on this property, this exit did not light up at all. All I could see was a small amount of tunnel that was lit by the light inside the elevator. Deciding I would have to explore this later, I pushed the button on number 2. The door closed, and the elevator began its methodical trip down the shaft.

The next stop was well lit, and I could see a short passageway with a small door inside the large one. I walked to the door and pushed the open button. Lo and behold, the passage opened with the roar of the tunnel vacuum starting and taking off down one of the passageways. I was on the first underground level of the "cellar," and for once in my many exploring travels underground, I knew where I was. A quick look around and back through the door I went and back to the elevator. I was sure the next stop would be the military floor as I had been known to refer to it to myself.

A short trip on the elevator proved my suspicion right, and I did see where this was located at the end of one of the log tunnels full of military equipment.

Enough of this business. I jumped back on the elevator and went to the top again, all the way to the top of the rock. The ride took about fifteen minutes, but was a lot faster than the four-wheeler. As I departed the old man's quarters and shut the secret door behind me, I hoped I hadn't disturbed anything for right now, so he would not know I was there.

I found my four-wheeler and jacket and slowly crept away as to not disturb the ground. The trip down the hill seemed to take forever, but my wife and dog were waiting for me when I arrived.

Over a cup of coffee, I related my journey of the morning. Amid many questions and concerns, the story unraveled, and some of the information about this place was revealed for the first time. After about an hour, we decided that was enough for a while and decided to figure out what we were going to do the rest of the day.

Chapter Forty-nine

I decided to do some investigation on my own and called the office to inquire if Ambrose would be available in the afternoon for a small trip. My secretary informed me he was out for the day and wanted to see if it were possible to wait until tomorrow. She reminded me I was informed about his absence a couple of days ago. Of course I remembered being notified as she was saying it. I told her what I needed could wait and hung up the phone.

With that out of the way, a trip down the tunnel to check out the vacuum machine was the next step. It was parked back where it belonged, and all was like nothing had happened. This seemed to satisfy me for the moment.

While thinking about all that happened, it dawned on me that the times I had heard the small chopper were the days when Ambrose was unavailable. In retrospect, it was about every two or three weeks he was unavailable, and every two weeks the past month. With that in mind, the plan was for me to stay outside and track the time of the return, if I could.

About seven o'clock, I heard the noise of the helicopter, quite faint, but still up there. The chopper spent very little time in the area, just enough time for a person to exit and get away from the blades before it was up and gone.

About forty-five minutes later, a call was received from Ambrose asking about the need of his services that day and wondering what time I would need him tomorrow.

An excuse that I had handled the need for the journey to town via a phone call instead seemed to relieve him of any anxiety of him being unavailable for the present time. He is a very dependable person and will do anything you ask; however, this seemed to create a problem in the back of my mind about his total trustworthy status.

This incident had taken my full attention all day and continued to bother me into the night. I kept thinking about all that happened since the first day I had arrived and the many things that were still unexplained. I had put my trust in all these people and was beginning to believe all of it may be a sham or a cover-up of something illegal, immoral, or impossible! I was realizing the only person I really felt comfortable with was the young man who arrived with the big horses. With nothing solved, finally about one o'clock, I fell asleep.

Chapter Fifty

Morning came very early after the late night. I had my morning coffee and took a stroll out through the corral area to look at the animals; seeing the horses always seemed to settle me down a little. My thoughts were interrupted by Mathew. He had walked up behind me without me hearing him. He apologized for startling me, and said he had good news.

Arrangements had been finalized for his fiancée to be brought out for a two-week stay. She would be accompanied by her older brother and a local neighbor who owned a car. If it was all right, they would arrive in a week.

I told him he had my blessings, and I would have my wife make the necessary arrangements for their room and board. They would be welcome to have a run of the place and enjoy their visit as much as possible. If needed, I would have Mathew's chores taken care of so he could have as much time with them as possible. If anything special was needed to accommodate them, he should let one of us know.

He assured me he could easily handle his responsibilities as well as entertain the visitors.

I returned to the house for breakfast and passed the word on to my wife; she was just enjoying her first cup of coffee. She was excited for Mathew and his bride-to-be and said she would hunt him down this morning to get all the information needed for an enjoyable visit.

With that business and breakfast handled, I headed to the office for some unknown reason. As I sat down at my desk, I noticed a neatly folded piece of paper on the desk. I slowly unfolded it, as if I thought it might blow up or something, to be greeted by a handwritten message:

I know you know I am here. Meet me at my quarters at ten o'clock. Come alone and don't tell anyone yet. You know the way.

The handwriting was the same as other notes I had found on my desk before in reference to "How he liked what I had done," etc. After a few seconds, I realized my heart was racing. I took a couple of long hard breaths to slow it down. That seemed to take longer than I thought it should. Finally, a walk outside was in order.

I passed my wife on the way out, and she said, "You look like you just have seen a ghost!"

I replied, "I am all right, just heartburn."

When the truth of this moment comes out, there will be hell to pay for that statement.

I walked toward the corrals again, but this time I found myself glancing up at the rock abutment high upon the hill. I had the eerie feeling he was probably watching me at this moment, just trying to see what type of reaction the note had created.

My heart slowed down to a mild roar, and finally I felt as if I had come to grips with what was about to happen. I had about an hour and a half before this meeting, and then I went back to my office to look over as much of the paperwork Christopher had left for me.

I picked up the note again and slowly read it through. It was such a long note, with nineteen letters, counting the punctuation marks. I did notice this time that there was a small letter toward the bottom of the paper, and it was the capital letter N.

Chapter Fifty-one

About nine thirty, I couldn't stand it any longer and started the trip into the wheel and make my way to the location of the tunnel vacuum parking spot. Before I left, I told my wife where I was going and not to worry. I told her if I didn't return before dark, she should call the office and send the "cavalry."

I did not hurry through the system, being more cautious than before, since I now knew there were other people who knew how to utilize the tunnels and doors. As I approached the location of the vacuum, it started and left the parking station long enough for me to enter the tunnel to the elevator that would take me to the top of the rock. The elevator was waiting for me. The elevator made the slow trip up to the top. When I arrived, the door opened to the well-lit tunnel, which I knew would take me to this man's housing arrangement.

Upon reaching the living quarters, I was greeted by a man with very thin gray hair and short stature. He was humped over, and I would guess he was about as tall as me.

"Good morning. My name is N. Fobias Bean. I am the person who sent you the note. Please sit down here, and I will start this meeting. It should take about two hours."

I sat where he had indicated, and he took an armchair across from me. I could see he had things set up for reel-to-reel movies, VHS tapes, and last but not least, DVD players. He seemed to have an agenda and was not going to waste any time with chitchat.

"As questions arise, I will answer them, and by the way, just call me N. We will be joined by Ambrose in a few minutes. There are some stuff I will tell you that he does not need to know."

With that tidbit of information, he started to tell the story of the Wheel Ranch, from start to the present.

"The Wheel Ranch started right after World War II. The Germans had a lot of programs going that the U.S. government wanted to check out, some to toss and some to continue on with. They brought a lot of the German scientists to the U.S. and dispersed them across the country to get all this information and pick and choose programs and scientists.

"There are, or were, twenty of these installations built—only three still exist in any form, and only this one is complete. This one's purpose was genetics and the idea of the 'superhumans.' I am the last of the test-tube babies, and as you can see, it didn't work well. I was born on the same day as you were, me here and you in the local hospital. We actually went to junior high together, and I tried to pick a fight with you. You told me you had to catch a bus because you lived in the country and wouldn't make the date. Later, we were cordial to each other and actually had some good conversations about boy stuff over lunch in the lunchroom."

He paused a moment to catch his breath and let that info soak into my thick head.

"This place was designed to sustain five thousand people for a period of at least five years and up to fifty as needed. You have seen the complete structure and probably think that would be impossible, but some of the things they invented, if sent to a very poor country in Africa, would end the hunger there. You ask, 'Why not send it?' The answer is it would also upset the world's economic system as well. This is not a concern if you are trying to survive an atomic disaster. That is why this was known as the Noah project.

"If you were to go to D.C. and mention the Noah project, only three men and one woman would have the faintest idea what you were talking about or really care. Congress does, however, continue to appropriate money to keep this place protected, thus, the military in the lowest level. The equipment is the newest stuff and is upgraded yearly. The food, as you well know, is current and the people that keep it so are offspring of the original people who set this up and are sworn to secrecy."

Another stop to gain his breath, this time he seemed a little paler than before. It also took a couple more minutes than before.

"Why don't you slow down a little and stop more often so you don't get so winded," I asked.

"I will try," he remarked.

"I am from the second round of babies, and I actually had a physical mother. She wasn't much to look at, but she took good care of me until I was fourteen. She passed away from the same type of illness that I have today. No cure. Passed on through generations. The genetic defect will stop with me as I was also born sterile. They weren't interested in any of my genes."

He gave me a small grin.

Another pause, but this time he had not gotten as excited as before in his commentary about the Wheel Ranch.

"Let's start at the front gate and work our way to the back. As Ambrose told you, the drive is a runway. It is designed to be able to land larger planes than you would think. It also has a catapult system to aid them on takeoff if needed. The gate itself is made to take a direct hit of explosives or by a tank and will not crumble. If a tank were to break the gate, sharp six-foot stakes with explosive heads will spring up and penetrate the heaviest armor plate. I wouldn't want to be inside the vehicle they hit.

"The main house, as you know, will recede into the ground and just leave the outer shell. The shell will take a direct hit from a small nuclear device before being destroyed. There are two other shells for the house down on the third floor of the main underground facility if their replacement is needed. The interior house itself, when retracted, will withstand a direct hit from a lot larger nuclear device. Everything under the ground here were made to withstand anything World War III would have to offer and more. Over the years, it has also been updated as new threats arise.

"The machine guns you have found in the trees are all automatic and have a long range as well as an up-close range. They have the capability of putting a bullet between your eyes at a range of a mile and a quarter. They are all synchronized together for maximum coverage. I didn't want to burst his bubble, but I had found antennas, but no machine gun nests.

"Three years ago, the army decided to test the security system. An all-out ground attack was planned and carried out on a quiet Sunday morning. They used rubber bullets and the troop of attackers numbered over two thousand. No one made it more than two hundred yards inside the fence without being hit. This security goes all around the main property and has been reactivated to surround the complete complex since you purchased it from your neighbors. I really do not know why they keep this up, because there are no top-secret things here. It may be a safe house for some government official, but no one has told us. All the operation of the compound's total security system is controlled from another location until local operators can be assembled and brought to this site. During the make-believe assault, it was never necessary for that to happen. In case of a breach, the off-site controllers can make all the local controls inoperable and unlivable conditions for a time. The place is very secure!"

"What happens to the people living here in case of a breach?" I quizzed.

"Before the breach happens, everything inside will be hidden and secure" was his reply.

"Located on the grounds and at strategic locations are missiles. They are tucked underground, and you could look forever and never find one unless it is being fired. They are regularly maintained, but you will never see that either.

"There is a group of four men that oversees this operation. You will probably never see them as they do not worry about the day-to-day operation of the property. They make ground-moving decisions like approving you and your family to inherit this. Do not let all this talk of guns, missiles, armies, security, etc., bother you. You own the property and can do what you want. Oh, by the way, great work on the two land purchases. With those, you have returned this complete compound to its original size. Someday, more than likely, the military will pull out of here, and you won't know they left.

"Christopher gave you a lot of information about the underground power generation and daily operational information. The repair of all the equipment will be taken care of until at least the year 2200 by contract, provided anyone is left by then. Keeping the first underground floor secret is not necessary, but probably to your advantage to keep lookie-loos away."

"The gold stash, what is with that? I damn sure don't need the money, but why is it stashed here?"

N chuckled and said, "That is a very good question. When they were constructing this facility, they hit a vein of high-quality gold. As they were not miners and were making a good wage, it was cemented in and forgotten by most. After this place started to close down from doing all the research, a couple of the original men decided to look for it. They found the vein and mined it as a pastime over a couple of years. They were not careful, and both died of mercury poisoning. Neither had any family, and the secret stayed here.

"Once in a while, I used to putter with the stuff, thus the safety equipment. I had nowhere to spend the money and no urge to leave the property. At three hundred dollars an ounce, there is just over a billion dollars there. How you could market it, I don't know, because the gold is of such pure quality it would raise a red flag when it hit the market, and this place would be crawling with people. This secret has gone to a lot of graves over the years, including Christopher's."

That thought hit pretty hard, and we both just sat there quietly for a couple of minutes. N was catching up on his oxygen intake and actually hooked a tube to his nose for some assistance of getting enough with each breath.

"What do you do and have done for the past however number of years you have been here?" I finally asked.

He removed the tube and started in again. "I was designated the overseer when I turned sixteen. I never had the need for companionship, and all I had to do was watch the comings and goings from my perch. It is quite amazing just how far you can see from here on a clear day. The pollution has diminished the view over the years, but it is quite spectacular to see after a snowstorm when all is clean for a while.

"This has been my home since then, and I have loved every minute of living here. As you can see, things are updated and comfortable. No real need for someone to live here anymore. The function has been replaced with surveillance equipment from afar. A personal suggestion, after I am gone: keep this place as a personal escape from the whole world when you need peace and quiet. I will leave all this information here neatly filed where you can browse it as you please."

"Today," he began, "there are two hundred people lined up to come here if there was an emergency that would require people to seek asylum from the outside. If given enough warning, the second level would become a small city with all the amenities. The third level would be filled with two hundred military types and what families they have. If enough time were given, you may want to think about a list of people you would like to save from death or danger. The amount of time allotted would of course depend totally on the amount of warning that was given. You will be warned as soon as anyone else who would be allowed to come here.

"Most of these people you have already seen or met. Some of the doctors and nurses are from the hospital and clinics, a couple of dentists, some law officials, and of course, Judge Gillipi. Also all the people from Smalliker Enterprise who have been cleared and some from a couple of the other businesses that are part of your financial world. All the predetermined people have an assignment and are checked out on that assignment yearly.

"People you bring in will be assigned a task after they have arrived, a task they are most fitted to do, for example, teacher. As much as you may not like, you will not be in charge at that time, but you will have a great amount of input. The Wheel still is yours until you give it away or sell it, neither of which I think you will do."

That thought did not sit real well with me as he said it, but after a little thought, it seemed to really make sense. "I would like to meet with this person in charge before there was ever a need to fill this place with people and someone telling my world what to do," I stated.

"That will not happen as it may change from day to day. They do not want you to become too friendly."

"They are?" I asked.

He only shrugged his shoulders.

The longer N talked, the more he started to remind me of Yoda from *Star Wars*. He talked along and stopped once in a while to gather his thoughts and catch his breath. He must have noticed the look on my face one time when he stopped, because he gave me a long look before continuing.

He placed a book about seven inches thick on the table. He said, "This book has all the operating and maintenance manuals for everything under the ground here."

After he set another almost as big there, he said, "This one tells of everything that was done or tried to do here. Don't read the second book before you go to bed. It may give you nightmares."

Another pause for a breath, and then he started the reel-to-reel movie. Most of it was the construction of the complete facility, all the tunnels, towers, buildings, cattle guard at the gate, drives, etc. This film showed nothing that I was not aware of, and I was starting to get slightly bored with it. As it ended, I asked N if we could step out and catch a breath of fresh air.

We exited the same way as I had entered a couple of days ago, and stood and let the fresh air into our lungs. The day was warm and beautiful, and it was nice to see nothing but nature for a minute. After seeing the reel-to-reel, it was amazing how much reclamation had been done. This whole region looked as if it had never been touched!

Chapter Fifty-two

"The rain and lightning storm the other night, didn't it shake the hell out of this place?" I asked.

"When these storms come in, I just go to the back of the apartment and read a book or work on a puzzle. It is impossible to watch TV or use the Internet with all the static electricity floating around. The bolts of lightning actually discharge into a couple of giant rods located a hundred yards from here that absorb the charge to reduce it to a useful commodity for storage to be used as needed later.

"I don't remember seeing any reference to that system," I quizzed.

"Christopher was open to and aware of a lot of the things that go on here, but was not let into the entire loop. Since he had worked for the government, he thought he knew it all and wanted it all his way. That was not going to happen while I was around!"

"Since you are leaving, is that why I am being told?" I quizzed.

"Partially, but you were to be told within six months anyway. Your contacts will not compromise the existence of this place as it would have if Christopher had been told. You returning this to a viable farm/ranch operation makes the disguise far more believable. You may notice changes in the lower tunnels that look like they may be retrofitted to accommodate the influx of people. Maybe someone knows something I do not!"

That statement took me by surprise, and both of us just stood in silence for a minute.

"Back to work," he said. "We still have a lot to cover."

The second session was on VCR tapes with excellent filming and color. It covered all the updates from where the reel-to-reel stopped, until about fifteen years ago. A lot of what was changed was due to new ideas on how things should be run and new technologies. It was quite boring to watch and listen to. It then went into some of the dark side of the wheel and the experimentation that went on here: some genetic engineering, good or bad or both; psychological experiments, some causing insanity and suicide; all kinds of crop changing and animal interbreeding, trying to see if they could breed a cow with a horse, etc. A little of this weird stuff went a long way. It did end by saying most of the experiments were a failure, and that was why this place was shut down or phased way back. Was I ever glad to get that one over!

The next phase was installed on a DVD and again was pleasant to watch. It showed a total restoration of the military equipment and the control centers. Changes were made so there was no signature of any kind that there is anything except a farm/ranch here.

"These were just finished last week," N stated, "right under your feet."

"Amazing" was my reply.

The show continued and showed a mock emergency of a virus pandemic. It showed how people would be allowed in and how long of a time they had to get here, a quarantine period, and approximately how long it would last. A little futuristic for my taste, but something I would have to give long thought to. There was a section about how all of this was detailed in very large manuals, with step-by-step instructions on how to do everything you would want to do in this installation. The final few minutes were an introduction of the four governing people and explained what they did and where they were.

After the completion of the filmed session, we were joined by Ambrose to finish up the session.

"I apologize for not being forthright with you, but it did not compromise my job as a bodyguard. I would have given my life for your protection since day one," Ambrose said.

I accepted his explanation and decided to leave it at that. "I hope neither of us ever gets to that point."

N started to explain he would be out of this apartment in two days and have it cleaned and sanitized. Ambrose would be in charge of that operation. N was going to a special place to finish his life in peace, all two or three days he had left.

He did not seem too bothered by the idea of death; I guess he had a long time to think about it. From the way he talked, the eventful day may be his choosing.

All the books, TVs, electronics, everything would be left. The bedding and furniture will be new as well as all linens and utensils. He suggested I come up here with my wife and watch the sunset in a few days; it is a very pleasant experience.

"Remember, I have now given you the resources to totally control what goes on here, with a little help, of course. Familiarize yourself with it, as the way this world is going, you may need to. Also remember you are under surveillance, and some really want to know what is going on here for their own gain. Those gentlemen in the black van are prime examples."

That was the one and only time I saw N, and as I headed back to the house through the tunnels, I thought how it would have been nice to spend more time together. He had put his whole life here and now was leaving for good.

Chapter Fifty-three

A few days later, I noticed the sound of the small helicopter coming in from the backside of the mountain. It appeared to stop briefly at the rock and then rise up and head toward the main house. As it flew over the house, it paused and lowered itself until I could see N in the passenger seat. He gave me a big wave, and then they were off, headed to some unknown destination, for a known ending.

I let a week go by and finally convinced my wife and dog to make the trip to the rock for a sunset. Neither liked the elevator ride, but they were getting used to it as we arrived.

As promised, the apartment N had occupied for years was spotless and well arranged for great comfort. It was a few minutes until the sunset would get wound up, and we slowly explored the entire area. There were many interesting items, such as rocks, crystals, a gold nugget the size of a grapefruit, maps, a very nice telescope and spotting scopes, shelves of hardback books by the hundreds, and much more.

We finally sat in two recliners that faced the west and watched the beautiful sunset. It almost took your breath away as N had promised. All of a sudden, I noticed a small card on the table between the recliners. Thinking it was N's idea of a joke, I picked it up. It read

I REALLY LIKE WHAT YOU HAVE DONE HERE.

KEEP IT UP. I'M WATCHING!

"K"

<u>K?</u>

I REALLY LIKE WHAT YOU HAVE DONE HERE.

KEEP IT UP. I'M WATCHING!

"K"

K?

Lightning Source UK Ltd.
Milton Keynes UK
UKOW02f2137260616

277067UK00001B/48/P